ALLYSON YOUNG

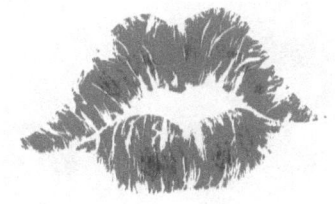

EVERNIGHT PUBLISHING ®

www.evernightpublishing.com

Copyright© 2018

Allyson Young

Editor: Audrey Bobak

Cover Artist: Jay Aheer

ISBN: 978-1-77339-696-5

ALLYSON YOUNG

BOUND BY DESTINY

Blue Star Shifters, 1

Allyson Young

Copyright © 2016

Chapter One

"Your twenty-fifth birthday is in a few months, River." Her sister Cassandra lazed across her bed, one long fingernail idly tracing the pattern in the comforter, but River wasn't fooled. The petite blonde—Cass was a brighter, prettier copy of River—was broaching a taboo subject, and it wasn't out of malice or prurient curiosity. Little sister was anxious, and River had to admit she had good reason to be. Cass was eighteen and the years tended to fly by, especially since she was aware of River's anxiety, something she didn't understand.

"I know when my birthday is, Cass. Which is why I'm packing up and taking a job on the other side of the country long before that day comes. Long before Dad decides to bring males by in order to test my suitability."

"You know our Alpha won't let that stand." Her sister didn't concede that their father had much say in the matter, and River winced inwardly. She had a complicated relationship with her dad.

"We don't know that for certain. It's the first time, to my knowledge, that any female has decided she's not going to toe the line and be mated against her will." One would think there had been others, but if so, no one spoke about them. Besides, once the male indicated his intent, the female went into heat—if they were compatible—and a choice was moot. So she wasn't taking any chances. River planned to leave at a time when there were the fewest of their pack about, and if no one stopped her, it was unlikely the Alpha would make a major effort to track her down. She hoped.

Cass wrinkled her nose and squinted. "You mean that. It would be against your will."

"I mean it." In fact, the idea made her stomach clench and her head pound. Being bound to some overbearing male wolf, powerless to naysay him, whether it be for sex or what he deemed fitting behavior for his mate, freaked her the hell out. Not to mention popping out as many offspring as he wanted for his clan. She knew all the single males in their pack and while she liked some of them—as friends—there wasn't one she could see herself mated to, especially as the remainder were either uncouth or callow. Mating would put them in charge and she shuddered harder at the thought. They could make her do anything...

"But what if you run into a lone wolf? Or there's some other pack in the place you're moving to, or thereabouts? They'll seek you out."

Evasively, River replied, "I've got a few ways around that, Cass. You'll just have to trust me on it."

Little sister frowned, but didn't press, instead tried to look at the issue from a different viewpoint. "Mom was okay with it. I mean, she went into her bind willingly and she and dad cared about one another." Cass's pretty face took on a hopeful cast.

River was of two minds about how willing her mother had been, but then she'd been older when Mom died. Cass likely didn't remember the not-so-happy times the way she did when their father had exerted his will and Mom didn't have a choice. She'd heard the noises her mom made, the begging and the pleading. Noises that caused River to pull the covers over her head and wish she could sleep as soundly as her sister. Not that she was going to say anything about it to Cass. Better her sister kept her good memories without taint.

"They did care," Cass insisted, and River realized she had been lost in thought. A shiver etched its way up her spine when she considered that any male who mated her could demand the same accommodation. It had spoiled her relationship with her father, building a distance between them. When he'd somewhat recovered from the loss of his mate, he initially tried to breach the gap with River, before obviously preferring his younger, less-resistant child.

"Of course, they cared," she proclaimed, injecting a sincerity into her voice she didn't feel. White lies were acceptable if it diminished her sister's anxiety and kept happy memories intact.

"He didn't seek out another mate after we lost her, because he was attached to Mom. Wolves want sons, River. And all he has is us. So it had to be his feelings for Mom that got in the way of accepting another mate."

River smiled and nodded. Maybe that was true. Her father never said, at least not to her. She frowned and then immediately erased it. Cass had to know what transpired between a bonded pair. All wolves did once they left childhood behind. It wasn't like the pack held secrets, but the way certain behaviors were couched as being normal and acceptable meant her little sister didn't view it the way she did. She thought everything was consensual.

River hadn't let her own perception spill over,

because until recently she hadn't figured out a way to avoid it. Another cramp hurt her belly. Perhaps she should tell Cass about her concerns sooner than later and not wait until she was established elsewhere and could send for her.

Before she could open her mouth, Cass gave her a watery smile and slipped from the bed, making her way to the door. "I'll start dinner."

It was interesting that she and her sister hadn't speculated beforehand. Why hadn't she thought that maybe her dad was too broken-hearted to mate again? *Because you can't fathom how a man could loan out his mate to other males and truly care for her. It isn't like the experimental sex a lot of the young wolves take part in. That you avoid.* She gave her head a little shake to dislodge all the fleeting thoughts. One thing was for certain—she wasn't having a conversation with her father about any of this. He'd already announced her fate from his point of view at the dinner table a few weeks ago.

"I'll be talking with Alpha Reeves, River. He'll have an idea who to send your way. I want grandchildren before too much longer, and you'll soon be of mating age."

Cassandra knew River planned to gainsay their parent, but could be counted on not to tattle. Sibling loyalty was strong in their household, seeing as River had stepped in when their mother died and their dad had foregone parenting at a time when they needed him the most. Even Cass's relationship with him, though more solid, hadn't recovered from his neglect.

Once again, she speculated. How much should she share with her sister as to why she was so resistant to being mated, aside from being placed in the subservient role in such an arrangement? Squeezing her eyes shut, she decided not to upset Cass further. It was enough she thought River was simply being independent, and there was enough time to rescue her sister.

She double-checked her list of items yet to pack. Her suitcase was tucked in the closet, away from prying eyes, though her father never set foot in his daughters' rooms. There were but a few things to add, and it would take only minutes to stuff them inside. And then she'd be out the door and on her way to the train station—in two days' time. She wasn't home free yet, but the relief of having a plan, well in advance of her birthday offered a modicum of relief.

As she put the list away, she heard the front door open and several male voices filled the air. River frowned. It wasn't poker night, or at least not her father's turn to host it. Smoothing her hair and straightening her shirt, she put a smile on her face and went to greet their guests. It was imperative everything appeared as normal as possible—until the day after tomorrow. If he'd invited people for dinner without letting either her or Cass know, something he tended to do, she wondered how she could help stretch the meal her sister would have started.

"River! My girl!" Reginald Fortuna beamed at her. She tried to hold her smile, but something in her father's face caused a tiny blossom of worry to burgeon. With a sinking heart, she recognized one of the other men with him—Jericho Reeves, their Alpha.

"Hi, Dad. Mr. Reeves."

"No need to be so formal, River. You'll soon be calling me Dad. Or maybe Father, if you prefer." Her Alpha smiled so widely she could see his canines.

A clatter behind her announced the fact that Cass had heard the pronouncement as a pot fell to the floor. River fought to keep her knees solid and cautiously ventured a look at the big male towering over both her parent and her Alpha. She took in his forbidding countenance and thick, black hair before realizing a pair of pale-blue eyes had scanned her from head to toe and probably read her thoughts at the same time.

Her wolf rolled over submissively and whined in response to a rolling wave of heat that scorched River's insides, and it took a huge effort to keep herself in check and show nothing other than a calm query. Wolves had a notoriously good sense of smell, but she trusted the supplements she'd been swallowing twice a day to manage her hormonal response, or at least to dumb it down. It appeared she'd been successful because those eyes narrowed slightly and her father looked confused.

So did her Alpha, who turned to stare at her dad. "I thought you said she was but a few months shy of her twenty-fifth birthday. Jett is an Alpha. And as such, highly potent."

"She'll be of age in under three months," her father muttered. He gestured toward the unnamed male. "River, this is Jett Reeves. He's come to our pack to take a mate. He has his own pack—Blue Star—but our Alpha is looking to cement ties. Jericho and I decided you are mostly likely the perfect choice, and so we brought Jett over. He just… That is, he staked his claim. But you…"

"She should have morphed, or at least shown evidence that she's nearly ready." Reeves senior frowned and stared as she struggled to cope with the information dropped on her. When had his son left Paradise? She knew all of her Alpha's offspring and wouldn't have forgotten a male such as Jett. Perhaps she'd been too young to remember. She was able to make a minimal response and hoped it distracted them from the fact she hadn't overtly jumped into her heat when Jett pushed his claim. "Welcome back. I'm sorry I don't remember you."

"I have never lived here. My mother and I, and

the rest of my pack reside several territories away." His deep voice was void of any inflection as River took in the surprising fact that a she-wolf had been allowed to live separate from her mate. But the Alpha had a mate here, too, and several, older mated sons...

"I didn't realize wolves could have two mates." The impertinent observation fell from her mouth before she could think better of it. Her father choked and her Alpha huffed.

"My mother isn't his mate. But Jericho has recognized me as his offspring and I've agreed that we become allied." Jett engaged her directly, ignoring the other males, and she was shocked by it. But then, he was an Alpha in his own right, apparently, and as such could make the rules.

She managed a tiny nod, shelving the mystery. Should she say something about being honored by the inference she was to have been the sacrifice to bind the two packs? She didn't think she could lie convincingly, so she stood there like a brainless idiot.

"Are there two more for dinner?" Cass piped up, moving to stand beside her, and the comforting press of her sister's hand gave her strength. "I'm Cassandra, River's sister."

"My *little* sister." She didn't miss the flash of amusement in those artic-blue eyes as Jett recognized her protective tone.

"We'll stay," proclaimed their Alpha. "We have some things to straighten out."

Her apparent lack of hormonal response was likely right at the very top of those things, as though there was something lacking in her. River knew she'd have to pop a few more pills before they sat down to dinner. "It will be ready in about half an hour."

Jett and Jericho nodded. Her father led the two

men toward the living room after casting River a baffled look. She could feel the shakes coming and willed the males out of sight, turning to follow Cass into the kitchen. He'd triggered her heat, but perhaps it wasn't full onset. She could only hope, because if not, the next while was going to be difficult. Traveling would be nearly impossible while hiding such urges. The symptoms would draw unwanted attention, especially that of other wolves. She cursed that Jett under her breath.

"What's going on?" Her sister hissed the words.

"Dad and our Alpha have decided to hand me over to an Alpha out of our territory." River couldn't keep her hands from trembling as she yanked open the freezer door and rummaged for more steaks.

"I thought that's what I heard. Oh, River. What are you going to do? It's one thing for you to move away on your own and yet stay in contact. If that Alpha takes you, I'll probably never see you again!"

"Shh. Don't even think that too loudly. I'll figure it out. We'll get through dinner. And then I'll leave first thing tomorrow."

Cass whimpered and wrung her hands. "So soon? I can't stand it…" The younger woman narrowed her eyes and tilted her head. "That Jett pushed his claim at you, River. *I* felt something and I'm years away from a heat. You didn't break a sweat, and you didn't… I mean, there was no uh, sexual response."

"I know." *Don't ask, please don't ask.*

With an excited clap of her hands, Cass said, "But that's great. If you didn't react, then you aren't compatible. That gives you a little more time at home."

"Well, if not him, they'll come up with another, especially now that Jericho will be intrigued. I'll be at the top of his list to get matched. So best I leave as soon as possible. But we need to get a meal cobbled together. Slice some potatoes and onions and lace them with butter and spices. We can microwave them while the steaks cook. I'll stick the frozen ones on first and set the table."

Wolves liked their meat blued, so everything should be ready in the time frame she'd set. The sooner she fed the men and dealt with the questions coming her way, the sooner she could see the back of them and get gone herself. Maybe leaving tonight wasn't out of the question. Panic welled and she tamped it down, knowing it would deplete her energy.

Cass hustled to prepare the potatoes and she lit the barbecue, pausing only to surreptitiously take another handful of supplements. She dry-swallowed them while on the privacy of the patio, knowing they would give her some ease, and breathed in a great lungful of air against the inevitable interrogation.

Jett Reeves was an impressive alpha male, and one any female wolf would lust after and willingly accept his claim, but River was fully aware that such a specimen would command a large following of single males. She wasn't about to be handed around like a party favor, and the thought of being separated from her small family forever—even including her father—made her want to hurl. Anything could happen in Jett's home and she wouldn't have a single person to support her.

"The potatoes are ready." Little sister's voice floated out from the kitchen.

River started. "Okay, thanks," she called over her shoulder, throwing the thawed steaks on and turning the others to sear the opposite side. Within a few minutes, the meat was done and she forked them onto a plate. They could rest while she set the table.

"Want me to call them?" Cassandra was back to looking nervous.

As the eldest, River should be the hostess, but she didn't want to rack up any brownie points. Jett needed to find her totally unsuitable. If she appeared lacking in social graces, an obvious requirement for an alpha's female, as well as not morphing into heat given his effort to bring it on, surely he would consider someone else. There were other females in her age bracket who were ready, and more importantly, willing to mate. It was ridiculous to experience a stab of disappointment that one of her peers would fall at his feet. "Sure."

Cass scampered off, and River took a seat as far away from where she assumed her father would seat Jett and her Alpha. She wanted the peace and quiet of her room to ponder the very different relationship Jett's mother had had with Jericho. She might even allow herself to think about Jett's rugged good looks, tall, muscled frame, and the way he'd almost stirred her. But that wasn't an option for now. Her wolf shifted uneasily beneath the masking layer of the supplements but remained acquiescent.

The men filed in and she pasted a vacuous look on her face, glad she hadn't changed her simple work clothing, though from the look her father shot her, she would hear about that later, in addition to anything else he regarded as behavior unfitting. The Alpha sat at the head of the table and after a little shuffling, her father went to the other end as Jett conceded it, taking a seat directly across from her. *Crap.*

To her surprise, the younger Alpha offered a quick blessing, in particular for the animal that gave up its life to provide them sustenance. Her assessment of him hitched up a notch, but she kept her eyes focused on her plate, thinking of her very nearly packed suitcase as the platters were passed around. The subsequent quiet was filled with the sounds of utensils against china while the food disappeared. Every morsel stuck in her throat as she braced herself for the questions that didn't come.

"Good meal." Jett spoke to both her and Cass, though how she knew that without daring to look at him was a mystery.

She murmured an acknowledgment and her sister echoed her. They didn't traditionally eat dessert, and she hoped that wasn't a requirement. Sipping at her water, she breathed slowly and steadily, and to the best of her ability ignored the male sitting across from her—the elephant in the room. Or more likely, *she* was the elephant, as well as her very un-wolf-like behavior. *Breathe. You'll be on your way in the morning. They won't like that you didn't respond, but they'll accept it.*

"Tradition dictates that a female who doesn't respond to a male's push isn't a suitable match." Her Alpha's announcement startled her and she jerked her gaze to him. He was glowering at her as though she'd spoiled his day.

"It doesn't happen very often." Her dad's tone held a hint of satisfaction, as though she'd finally become someone he could relate to.

"Very rarely," Jett weighed in, and she indeed felt the burden of his stare, so heavy she quailed beneath it and felt her lips quiver. "Perhaps she is late to mature."

She was right in the freaking room, at the same table. River bit her lip to refrain from saying something to interest any of the males, like acting vastly *immature* by indulging in some name calling. Or targeting a head with the handy salt shaker.

"That could be it." Her father didn't sound convinced.

"You could return and try again," suggested Jericho. "Closer to her birthday."

Jett shook his head and she shook with relief, until he added, "With your leave, Jericho, I'll take her with me and give our connection time to morph over the next while. If she isn't suitable, I'll return her personally. But I can't be away from my pack for much longer. Not with the unrest in the region."

"He came at my request because I truly thought your daughter a good match," Jericho advised her father. "Even if it wasn't a precipitous time."

Cass thankfully asked the question burning River's tongue, both of them knowing it would do no good to protest the move of a female when her parent and her Alpha approved. "When would my sister have to go?"

With a lift of one massive shoulder, Jett sealed her fate. "I'd planned to leave first thing in the morning, but tonight would suit me better."

"No! Daddy, please. It's too quick. River's been everything to me. Can't you ask for a little time?"

Tears pricked hard, but River refused to let them fall. Cass was doing what she couldn't, and all she could do was sit passively and pray.

"If you'd wait until the morning? The two girls are close, especially seeing as their mother died when they were so young." Her father actually entreated the younger Alpha and hope sparked for an instant. She only needed a few hours to put some distance between her and this place. And no alpha would follow when so obviously scorned. River could never come back after such a heinous act, but that suited her, especially when she could help Cassandra in the end.

"I'd like to speak with River. In private." Jett's tone was rife with something she couldn't interpret.

"Certainly. Use my study." Her father gestured down the hall.

Jett levered to his considerable height and she somehow stood and made her feet move. She led the way, glumly intuiting it might be the last time she would walk in front of him. Females followed, and it made her grit her teeth at what that inferred. The door to the street beckoned in her peripheral, but she'd never outrun the predator striding behind her.

The heavy panel shut behind them and she stepped behind a chair, casually positioning it so she could maintain a little distance.

"They aren't working as well as you think, River. You've fooled your father, and mine, but you responded to my intent to claim. Your heat will soon be apparent because I don't intend to allow you to take any more of those banned substances." His calm pronouncement was quiet but rang in the enclosed space nonetheless.

She could play the innocent or cut to the chase. A certain coiled strength was evident in his posture, but she didn't feel threatened. He looked implacable, as though he had all the time in the world. Despair washed over her and she clutched the back of the chair for support. His face softened and he motioned to it.

"Sit down before you fall down."

Leaning on the arm she slipped around and half fell into the seat, bitterly acknowledging she was already doing his bidding. "Why didn't you say something right away?" she asked.

He pulled another chair to face her, and when he sat, at least she didn't feel as though he was looking down on her from a great distance. He stared into her eyes. "I was intrigued that a female wolf would go to such lengths to avoid being mated, especially when your age dictates your destiny. And I wanted to talk with your father and obtain his understanding of his daughter."

She took a deep breath. While she was throwing a

meal together, he was gathering information. She wondered what her father had to say, and decided it had to be fabricated, because why else would this male want to take her with him?

He sat patiently, as she thought through her options of exactly... none. In that event, so what if she said all she had to say? What else could happen? There might even be a slight chance he would reject her. Getting through her heat unfulfilled would be hellish, but she'd find a way around that too. "I don't choose to be mated. I never want to fulfill such a destiny and be a second-class citizen for the rest of my life, used and mistreated for the perpetuation of the species."

His wide brow furrowed. "We'll discuss the latter part of your statement in a moment when I've had time to process it. But as to your determination not to mate, there are very few females who reject being mated. In fact, the only ones I'm aware of are— Are you ... disinterested in males? Or perhaps interested in both sexes?"

"No. I'm disinterested in sex, period." It wasn't true. She could admit, if only to herself, to having ridiculous romantic fantasies brought about by certain novels she and Cassandra read. Except her life was so far from that fiction...

"Your scent disproves your disinterest."

Lord, he had definitely scented her momentary lapse, even if the others hadn't. His father had called him potent, but she had come this far and wasn't going down without trying to dissuade him. "I'm a healthy, nearly twenty-five-year old female shifter, Jett." Maybe she should have called him Alpha, but he didn't correct her, not in words or with a censuring frown. "It's nature that my body—my wolf—would respond to your claim—or that of another. That doesn't mean *I* want to mate."

His tiny growl appeared to emanate from deep in

his chest and she blinked. He made no outward sign so she dismissed it as hearing things, and when he said nothing, she continued, "I simply wished to live a different life. Different from other females, different than my mother's."

"I can't speak to the relationships of all shifters, and certainly not ones within other packs, but perhaps you'll find things different within mine." He again spoke calmly and quietly, as though soothing a frightened child.

"So you've decided for me. You're taking me with you as your mate without considering my feelings on the matter." Despite her efforts, her voice was shrill. Desperate.

His black hair shone beneath the overhead lighting as he shook his head again. "Females are destined," he repeated, "and you responded to my claim. My father recommended you after careful consideration, and I agree with his choice. I have claimed you, despite the supplements you utilized to rebuff a claim and mitigate your heat. Surely you can accept that—as a she-wolf. Your mother must have educated you."

His arguments meant nothing. They couldn't mean anything. "I was only ten when she died, but, yes, she ... educated me as much as fitting for that age group. And as I got older, there were no secrets in the pack as to what the destiny of a female is, and that of the male. Unfair and inequitable as they are."

"You deem the male's need to dominate and protect his mate as unfair? Inequitable? What of the female's power? To meet her mate's needs as no one else can and also bring life?"

She snorted. "All diminished by mistreatment and being used."

"Your father did this?"

Color flooded her face at his quiet question. She

couldn't bring herself to reply.

"River, did your father abuse your mother?"

"I don't know you. I'm hardly going to confide such personal things in a stranger." Tears burned and she blinked furiously to hold them at bay.

"I'm your mate and who better than someone you can put your utter trust in?"

"Trust is built. And gained. I just met you!"

"I chose not to reveal your subterfuge to the others. I plan to take you with me tonight to spare you the indignity of being found out. And Jericho will determine what you've been doing, believe me, if I leave you behind until later. I've also chosen not to punish you for that behavior in front of your Alpha and your father, or in front of the pack. Is that not sufficient incentive to at least trust I have your best interests at heart?"

"Punish me?"

"You've broken a serious clan law and you well know it. I will administer a punishment."

"Such as?" Her heart rate sped up and she felt queasy. She knew what her pack's Alpha would order, but had gone ahead and taken the supplements anyway. She considered them a justifiable risk.

"A physical one, little River, so you can make amends and it will pass. At a time of my choosing, but away from here. Given your antipathy for mating and your obvious desperation, it will remain between us. Any further such transgressions may not."

And there it was. He was going to beat her, hurt her, just as Jericho would, although that man would order his minions to do it. Jett was no different, as much as he liked to pretend with his oh-so-thoughtful *I won't let your father or my father know what you've done* commentary. It was about his ego and losing face in front of Jericho. She shrugged. "Whatever. Do your worst."

His handsome face hardened before those icy eyes became thoughtful. "You expect the worst, my mate. You've resigned yourself and that's a shame. You have a right to expect better and live a long and happy relationship with me. And our pups. But you'll have to make it what you will. I'm a fair male, as you'll soon discover."

Enigmatic didn't suit him. But then he had all the power and she was doomed to live the very thing she'd intensely schemed to avoid. The thought of Cassandra undergoing the same process in a few short years made her choke on a sob. Jett reached out his hand and she flinched away, too upset to decipher the reaction that flashed across his features. "Am I allowed to say goodbye to my sister?"

"And your father."

"He doesn't matter, but Cassandra does. She was upset enough that I was leaving, let alone now I'll be someplace she'll never see me again."

"Where were you going, little River?" His tone was extremely quiet.

Well, she'd fessed up without even thinking. Stupid. All the more reason for him to punish her. "I'd planned to leave here shortly. I had a job and a place to live. It took me a long time to plan it out, but I did it. Cass could have joined me once I got established and made her own choices too."

"Would you have married a human?" There was something palpable in the question, but again she couldn't read him.

"I hadn't thought about it. Maybe. Anything to avoid *this*." Tactful she wasn't, but he was already going to take his pound of flesh, so whatever. She wished he wouldn't sit so close. The extra dose wasn't working well at all, and her wolf was barely constrained. Sweat beaded along her spine and her temples pulsed.

"Well then, I'm glad I came along before you escaped. A female wolf among humans isn't ... ideal, and there are certain repercussions, though you don't seem to realize that. I'm beginning to think your education has been sorely lacking in many areas. I'll assist you in your packing so you don't inadvertently throw in anything you shouldn't."

The last thing she needed was some arrogant male presuming to lecture her on shifter mores and laws when she'd done her best to live beneath the radar and spend most of her time with humans. "I'm packed. Except for the supplements—that I won't need—and a few sundry articles. But by all means, hover. I'd better get used to it."

In truth she wanted to scream and throw things at him, anything to distract herself from the eroding control over her hormones. At this rate, his pervasive claim would send her into a full heat before they departed her house, and how humiliating would that be? She'd seen the way female wolves acted when overcome by great need, and she wanted to avoid that at any cost.

Jett actually chuckled. "Get your case, feisty one. If I find anything that shouldn't be there, you'll rack up another punishment. And I keep all my promises. In the meantime, I'll speak with the others and inform them of our plans."

She rose from her seat, careful not to increase their proximity, knowing he was fully aware of her avoidance and amused by it. Damn him. Females were driven, ruled by their heat, and males, while vastly affected, were far more in control. It was nature because someone needed to ensure the female's safety as she lost herself. River hated him and her life and her species, not that it would change anything. But the thought of losing herself to him in the coming hours was making her crazy, and not with lust. Yet.

Passing through the living room on the way to her bedroom, she ignored the looks coming her way. Cass got up as if to follow but was called back by Jett. River quit listening to whatever he was telling them. It wasn't as though she had any say, and she wouldn't see them again in any event. Her heart crumbled and she hurriedly scribbled a note to her sister. She told her that nature had caught up to her before she could act any differently and that Jett had promised to be kind. Not a little white lie, but she couldn't let Cassandra fret. Let her believe that River's first heat dictated her actions as with all the other female wolves. Cass would understand that and it would assuage the loss to some degree.

Considering the container of banned supplements, she pried the top off and poured them into the toilet, salving her conscience about polluting the environment with a reminder they were all natural sourced and could return to the earth. She knew she was focusing on the strange and the mundane and couldn't draw out her leave-taking much longer. Jett wouldn't allow it—she knew that about him already.

She crushed the container beneath her heel and buried it within the garbage, and then disposed of the lid in a small box of odds and ends she couldn't bring herself to dispose of. Cass mustn't find any evidence in the event River was found out. Then little sister could truthfully state she had no idea her big sister was circumventing pack law. A rippling shudder of need nearly overtook her and she grasped the edge of the dresser for support. It was happening. To her. She swallowed another sob and focused on the task at hand.

Adding her e-reader and her reading glasses, she

took one last look around the small room she'd grown up in before picking up the picture frame that had sat on her dresser for as long as she could remember. Her mother's smiling face looked out at her, arms around her daughters. River searched that smile, wondering how the woman she both missed and resented hid the darkness of her life so effectively, before carefully putting the photograph into her case.

Despair and glum acceptance welled up to dampen her heat and she stood, stock still and barely breathing for a moment, until she became inured enough to push past it. She'd tried to find her own way, and being stopped so close to her goal crushed her. Her upbringing wasn't lost on her. Once Jett mated her, she was destined as his partner, if a silent, unequal one, and from that, there was no escape.

Shoving her phone in her back pocket, she grabbed her luggage and hauled it down the hallway. Jett came quickly to relieve her of the burden. "Are you ready?"

Would she ever be ready? Not in her lifetime, but it didn't matter. "Yes."

"That was quick," her father laughed. "You must be hopeful Jett is your intended."

So Jett was continuing to spin the farce that they would wait and reassess when she was closer to her birthday. River supposed she should be grateful that as promised he hadn't outed her and given a reason for an investigation. She didn't spare her father a word, focusing on Cassandra. She hugged her sister and whispered that everything was absolutely fine, honest. With a wolf's keen hearing, everyone in the room knew what she'd said, and both her father and Jericho smiled widely. Jett never took his gaze off of her—she could *feel* him watching and her wolf stretched languidly, then rolled and showed her belly.

"Really?" Cass searched her face. "You're sure?"

"Your sister will be fine. She'll call you soon and … if things work out and she stays, you can visit once she's settled. If your father and Jericho concur."

River spun and stared at Jett. It was unheard of for a young, unmated female to travel, let alone to another pack's territory. But he stared back and didn't retract his comment. Jericho and her father also remained silent and she dared hope that meant consent. She turned back to her sister. "See? It's fine. I love you, Cass."

"Love you more."

Jett touched her arm and she shivered, the call of his claim pulling her wolf so close to the surface she winced. The other males were standing taller, and appearing tense, and she accepted it was only a matter of minutes before they knew her to be claimed.

"Time to go." Jett urged her toward the door.

Cassandra squeezed her hand and swiped at tears with the other. "You call as soon as you can."

"I will."

"Be a good girl, River." Her father looked woebegone as he moved to stand beside her sister. He didn't try to approach, having eschewed touching her for years. Or maybe she'd rejected his touch so often he had come to refrain. "I'll miss you."

"Goodbye." She could hardly stand to say it, but she forced the farewell out and managed a nod in his direction.

"I'll be in touch, Father." Jericho acknowledged his son but said nothing to her, and River counted that as a small mercy, having expected some ribald comment.

Jett ushered her outside and to a huge black SUV crouched at the curb. After tossing her case in the back, he handed her into the passenger seat and ensured she was belted in securely. Perhaps he thought she would make a run for it, or hurl herself from the vehicle going at top speed. If it weren't for Cass, the latter might have been an option, but he'd offered the carrot of contact, and she was going to hold him to it. She recognized an honorable male when she met one, even if he was stuck in the pack mentality of believing in nature and destiny.

The powerful engine turned over and she leaned her head back against the leather seat. It seemed her mate had funds unless he was up to his eyeballs in debt. Time would tell. Emotionally drained, she hoped he wouldn't lecture her the whole way, and peered out her window into the deepening dusk. She couldn't possibly spar with him and fight the strengthening physical attraction at the same time. Her temples ached and her left leg jumped in place while her foot beat a tattoo against the floor mat.

Her entire body was extremely aware of him as a virile male—her mate—and her wolf was now wide awake, pacing, and clawing to escape. Her structured mind, an accountant's, was somewhat up to the task of maintaining a reserve, but only if she could focus.

"If you can sleep, do so. We won't be stopping for the night. I'll find a motel for a meal and a few hours' rest tomorrow. I know you are warring with your heat, but relax as much as you can. This isn't the time or the place to consummate our connection."

Her face heated in reaction to his clinical comment. Connection. Naturally, he knew she was unraveling, and playing the gentleman only made her more fragile. Why couldn't he have shown up two days late? Or not at all? A tear escaped and meandered down the rounded plane of her cheekbone before drying in the cool air emanating from the vents.

She closed her eyes, carefully angling her face away from a casual glance. Pretending to drift off, she slipped deep into her head, creating and solving difficult mathematical problems. It served to distract her wolf a tad, and she worked at it fiercely. Giving a little thought to her punishment cooled her ardor as well. When she had thought about her dad not touching her, it included no corporal punishment, so she was actually pretty scared of what Jett planned to visit on her. She'd noted the supple black belt he wore, and his hands were huge.

The big engine powered them on into the night, as she did her math and worried, the quiet, formidable figure at her side a forever reminder of her so called destiny.

Chapter Two

Jett pushed the SUV hard, viscerally aware of the sweet bundle of she-wolf strapped in beside him. Her wafting scent was increasing infinitesimally, despite her clear efforts to resist him, and it was driving him insane. Had he ever desired a female in this manner, even before pushing his claim?

He'd obeyed his sire's edict and attended his territory to appraise the suggested mate, not really believing she'd be suitable. And then River had appeared, a small, slight figure, dressed casually, the length of her body concealed. She'd done nothing with her hair nor used any makeup that he could determine, and yet she'd shoved past his defenses without effort— and apparently without knowing it. His reaction had been out of control, nearly annihilating the shield of the substances she'd ingested before he'd yanked it back in time to give them both space to breathe. And for him to ponder his decision.

Not that he'd considered refusing to claim her, not for a moment. He'd instinctively wanted to protect her from the wrath of the other males should they discover her perfidy, and to plan his strategy once he found out why she was so damn resistant. His father wasn't any help when it came to supplying information, either. Jericho never looked past destiny, although if anyone should, he'd be the one, but that was an issue for another time. In the end, River's father was simply elated that his daughter had caught the eye of an alpha with a good reputation, and Jericho was optimistic.

He knew his role and what was expected of him as Alpha. His father had left a council of six to teach and train him into that role, sometimes by dint of boots and fists. When he'd gotten older, he'd fucked a wide swath through all available females, both human and shifter, his sexual appetite little different than most of his peers. But none had stirred him the way River Fortuna did. Having seen clear and irrefutable evidence of destiny, her strong desire to avoid a predicted—and safe—fate puzzled him. And she viewed it as one sided. Whatever transpired between her father and mother obviously soured her on a claiming, and he wondered if that relationship had truly been unbalanced as she indicated.

Once they mated, he would be as bound to her as she to him, and that meant for life. Her father hadn't searched out another mate after her mother's death, and unless something vastly different had come to pass within Jericho's pack, Jett could only interpret his future father-in-law's reticence as an indication he remained devastated by his loss. So perhaps there was something else operating in River's head.

The man had relatively little to share about his daughter, but not out of reticence. Indeed, Reginald appeared unable to offer anything other than the most superficial information. If there was a question about how connected the two were, the way she ignored him at her leave-taking painted a clear picture. Jett suspected she had scant use for males, but he was up for a challenge.

Squinting at a shadow hovering at the edge of a ditch, he prepared to brake if the deer broke for the other side, but it remained stationary until they flashed past. River stirred slightly and his cock pressed painfully against his jeans. He doubted they could wait until returning to his territory and considered the choices of lodging ahead. There were a few pleasant, even luxurious, places to stop, though he doubted she would care. Yet he wanted nice surroundings for her.

He couldn't actually spare the time required for a proper claiming. As it was, the rogue wolves sniffing around his territory would have likely determined he was away and might press the advantage. But he'd never last until they got to his home, and more importantly, he doubted River would either, given that the supplements would be losing all effectiveness by now. A female's heat could be excruciating unless relieved, so he'd take her and mark her, albeit hurriedly.

A bit of remorse that he'd caused her sexual distress flickered through his head before he dismissed it. It was how pack life played out, and one little female couldn't change the eons of history. Once again he cursed his duty for interfering with a more leisurely courtship and vowed he'd make it up to her when they were home. Where he could show her the true nature of a claiming. Caring and affection grew from the physical connection and he intuited that it would be no hardship in feeling softer emotions for River.

After an interminable length of time, he spotted the turn off he remembered and slowed to take the service road. River sat up and her long blonde hair swung in ghostly patterns by the light of the dash symbols. "Are we there already? It's still dark." Her voice was strained and the strength of her heat was tangible. His dick, already strangled in his jeans, warred with his wolf to break free.

"This is a good place to stop and dawn will break soon."

"Are you tired?"

He nearly chuckled at the hopeful note in her voice. Given her distaste for a claiming and what he sincerely hoped were skewed ideas, perhaps she believed he required rest instead of—her. All of her. "I'm not tired."

"Oh."

He pulled the vehicle into the large parking lot and shut it down, and then turned to face her. "I've set my claim, River, and there's nothing to do but move forward."

"You've set your claim and I'm to follow along. Like I have any choice." The increasing sensual discomfort of her body was now evident in her tone and he avoided taking deep breaths, fearing her scent would overwhelm his more gentlemanly instincts. She already feared her future. He could smell that too.

"You don't," he said agreeably. "But I'll make it good for you."

She didn't reply, but the scent of her fear increased. Jett swore inwardly as he climbed out and retrieved his duffel and her suitcase.

River clambered from the SUV, reluctance imprinted on her every move, even as he marked her visible need. Jett herded her along, unable to touch her because of the bulk of the cases, which was probably a good thing. She paced toward the lobby and he admired her slender form, her wealth of hair spilling around her shoulders and down her back. He itched to feel the strands between his fingers and wondered what her wolf form looked like. Was she a pale wolf to his dark? Not that it was likely he'd ever know. River should never have a cause to shift.

Pressing the automatic door button so he could enter before her, he could feel her hesitate behind him and his wolf-self wished she'd bolt so he could shift and run her down. Mate her in the wild like his ancestors. A growl caught in his throat and he heard her whimper, and then follow him into the brightly lit foyer.

"One room. King-size bed. Jacuzzi if there's one available." River might like the benefits of a whirlpool.

"Certainly, sir. Have you stayed with us before?" The brunette manning the reception desk was gorgeous and put together despite the lateness of the hour. She left him cold, another indication that his claim was dead certain. Smiling charmingly, she ignored River who shuffled in place a fair distance away. "Ah, no Jacuzzi, but a steam shower is available."

Setting his burden down, he drew his wallet out and passed over a premium card. The woman's eyes widened along with her smile. "Thank you, sir."

He waited impatiently as she imprinted a plastic key and handed it over in a cardboard sleeve with the room number noted on it. Shoving it in his shirt pocket, he collected the luggage, jerking his head toward the elevator. River moved in that direction, her small frame visibly trembling, and he hurried to block the view from the receptionist. There was nothing he could do about her tiny moans, likely beneath the range of human hearing in any event.

They rode the elevator to the sixth floor in near silence, the eddies of lust making the small space nearly insufferable for him, and his mate leaned against the wall as though she might slip to the floor any moment. Her brow and temples glistened with sweat and her fingers twitched spasmodically. She was coming into her full heat and fighting it all the way.

Stepping off when the doors opened, he strode in the direction the small arrow indicated and found the room within several yards. The key card gave them entrance and he flicked on the light. He shoved the cases just inside the door, blocking the heavy panel with his forearm so it wouldn't close. "In you go, River."

Did women trudge? His woman did, despite the trembling of her entire body. His heart ached at her trepidation despite the all-encompassing lust he experienced. Her head down, intense need radiating to pull him in, he threw the deadbolt, and then gave in to what their nature decreed.

Thrusting his hand through her thick mane, his fingers weaving among the long, silky strands just as he'd fantasized, he drew her head back and forced her to look him in the eyes. Hers were dilated, the rich brown irises nearly eclipsed by the stark black of her pupils. Square, white teeth clenched her full bottom lip, presumably to control panting, because she drew draughts of air in through her nose. He could detect the threads of resignation weaving through her vast need, her intense heat rapidly eclipsing any coherent thought. Regret that he'd caused this again pierced his own narrowly shrinking focus—but only briefly. He lowered his head and took her mouth.

Sweetness and life burst over his senses at his first taste, and he groaned against her full lips even as his tongue made a foray past them. River totally surrendered, as female wolves do when they met their fated mate, and he barely had time for that thought—*fated mate*—before he wrapped an arm around her limp form. Two steps and they fell to the big bed, the mattress compressing beneath their combined weight as he ravished her mouth. She opened to let him in and gave up all the flavor that was uniquely her.

He reluctantly tore his lips away to rear up and shred the plain shirt that hid her from his view. Her lightly tanned skin filled his vision as her utilitarian bra met the same fate, and he noted with pleasure how modest her tan lines were. His wolf rose up. *Mine.* The growling claim resounded in the room and her eyes fluttered open and she blinked. Behind the thicket of her dark lashes, a sexual haze again blurred the rich chocolate, and her lids drifted shut.

Once they came to know one another, their coming together could be slowed and savored, but for now, he needed to visibly establish his claim. His frantic cock shuddered in agreement as he demolished the tough denim of her jeans, taking care not to score her soft skin with a claw.

With her nude beneath him, his gaze drawn to the soft, pale fur at her apex, he willed his other-self back, and his claws retracted. Lord knew what she'd seen when she'd stared up at him. Probably a wild-eyed beast intent on its succulent prey, and he blessed the Mother and the mating heat that River hadn't screamed in fear. Only an alpha could partially shift, and it was unlikely she'd seen one in that state before.

His own apparel fell away as he quickly stripped and then blanketed his mate's writhing form. Velvety flesh met his own in a haze of heat and sensation.

"Please." Her plea was strangled and all the more evocative because of it.

"I'll take care of you," he promised. "Always."

River whined and arched into him, rubbing her swollen breasts with their tightly bunched nipples against his chest. Her sex perfumed the air and her wet folds caressed his cock as she begged for him to release her from her sexual agony. Nearly mindless himself, he dipped his head to take a tender tip between his lips, marking how it elongated as he worked his tongue over the areola. River's small breasts were delectable, full and round, sitting high on her narrow torso, and he wished for another mouth as he abandoned the turgid nipple to seek out the other.

He longed for a taste between her thighs, but his cock was seeking out her entrance with a mind of its own and he succumbed to the call. Reaching to pull her thigh over his hip, he opened her to the broad head of his dick and advanced into her body. She was insanely tight, despite the welcoming warmth of her natural lubricant, and he applauded the scalding warmth as he plumbed into her depths.

The thin membrane guarding her gate gave way against his determined thrust and River tensed, ceasing her instinctive movements. He somehow stilled and waited as she adjusted to what was obviously her initial foray into sex. Few female wolves maintained their virginity and it wasn't a requirement. Both sexes sowed their oats before being claimed and they gained experience and understanding as a result. The comparison served to highlight the enhanced connection of a mating—casual copulation had none of the spiritual connection. But River had avoided even casual sex... Even as the thought flashed through his head, both he and his wolf growled their approval of being her first.

She relaxed as her heat once again directed her need and he concentrated on using slow and even thrusts until he was sheathed fully in her clenching pussy. River thrashed her head as he worked his arms beneath her to hold her close, reveling in the sensation of his true mate.

He spoke against her temple, holding her face against his neck. "Feel me, sweetheart. Just feel."

Slowly, she calmed, only tiny shivers apparent on her small frame. His skin pricked in response and he carefully lowered her head to the pillow. With every increasing movement, he pistoned in and out of her tight passage and heard her whimper, but this time with pleasure.

The base of his spine tingled in warning as he rutted between her widely spread thighs and she met him thrust for thrust in wild abandon. Forcing a hand between them, he sought out the cord of her sex, the tiny nub thrusting from its hood. No surprise, she shrieked at his touch, her clit so sensitive a gentle rub tumbled her over the abyss.

Pulling out, he flipped her onto her belly, lifting her into position with a grasp on either hip. He pushed his cock in deep, finding his way unerringly, yet fighting for territory against the swollen tissues resulting from her orgasm. He followed her into climax in a mere three thrusts, holding hard against her as his seed flowed with painful intensity from his balls, jetting from his cock and against the mouth of her womb, the walls of her channel flinching spasmodically around him.

Without hesitation, he set his teeth at the juncture of her neck and shoulder, his lips marking the silky skin there, and bit down. Instinct now drove him, for he'd never marked another, and the sweetly metallic taste of her blood sang through his being. His orgasm drew out to an almost painful degree, and then River cried out and he soothed the bite with his tongue. "Shh. You're mine. It won't hurt for long. Easy, sweetheart."

As a first claiming he would never forget it, and he knew she'd also been carried along on fulfilling sensation. He carefully withdrew on a flood of their combined secretions and River sobbed into the pillow. Jett realized she hadn't made any effort to hold him, despite his decision to initiate her with the tried and true missionary position. Indeed, her fists were still clenched at her waist. He stood in awe at her absolute determination to resist a claim—his claim—even in the throes of her heat.

His mouth set as he considered the myriad of difficulties ahead and the wonder faded in the face of it. He had enough to manage with his pack and the encroaching threats, let alone deal with such a recalcitrant mate. River would service him thoroughly and often and he wouldn't ignore her pleasure at any time. And hopefully conceiving his child would make her more amenable. But he was fast losing patience—

He brought himself up short, recognizing it was his ego pushing and making him react in such a manner. Somehow he would have to convince her that this was *right*, especially when he determined all of her needs and showed her he would meet them. Nature would prevail, after all, as a welcome ally.

Crossing to the bathroom, he soaked a washcloth in warm water before wringing it out and taking it back to gently cleanse her. He flinched at the sight of her virgin's blood while his wolf arched its neck—Jett the man could admit a certain satisfaction to being her first, knowing he wouldn't hurt her that way again.

She curled onto her side and made a querulous complaint, but was clearly in deep slumber. He looked his fill, the slight curve of her hip flowing to long, toned thighs and strong calves, tapering to slender ankles and manicured feet. Impulsively, he touched the pale, pink sparkly polish on her little toe. The pedicure seemed to be River's only concession to girliness and it made him smile.

Her long, blonde locks obscured her face in a mess of tangles, and he noted the myriad of shades enhancing them. He smoothed them back to admire her pert nose sprinkled with freckles and the wide bow of her lips, now slack as she slept. Her arm was folded over her chest, veiling her breasts, similar to the manner in which her thighs now shielded her sex. Even in sleep, she retreated, and with an inner sigh he tugged the covers free and drifted them over her recumbent form.

Snapping off the light, he set his mental clock to awaken him in a few short hours. He knew he'd want to have River again before they hit the road, but considering her recent virgin status, he resolved to put his needs aside. Maybe take care of himself in the shower, unless she required him again.

He lowered himself beside her, his heated body not requiring a covering, and hoped the thin barrier of the sheet and blanket would remind him of his most recent resolution when he woke. He wasn't anywhere near sated and he'd likely be in that shower more than once in a very short period of time. Despite being tortured with such close proximity, he rolled to spoon her and snuffled against the back of her neck, the rapidly healing bite an additional reminder of the way this female had imprinted on him. And he on her.

Chapter Three

River woke to the sound of water running. The surrounding smells alerted her to the fact she wasn't in her own bed, in her father's house, with her sister Cass about to come storming into the room, telling her to get up and make her famous pancakes. A heartsick pang for the loss of the familiar stole her breath before she cautiously sat up, pushing the bedding away.

She was naked, she who was so modest and always wore pajamas to bed. Not to mention she was a total mess. She could feel the places where her skin had been chafed by Jett's stubble, and the area between her legs throbbed. His scent was all over her, and a drift of her fingers against her neck determined a thinly raised area. He'd bitten her and the initial claiming was over. She wasn't thinking about the actual sex part of it, not that she remembered much more than being powerless in the face of her heat and Jett's big body covering her own. And denial was not only a river in Egypt.

The insane need had diminished to a simmering ache, but from what she knew of wolf heat, it wouldn't be long before it would require sating again. It was disgusting, being a slave to one's hormones, and the way to satisfy them wasn't something she wanted. Maybe if she kept telling herself that and dug ever deeper into denial... She ground her teeth in frustration.

Wrinkling her nose, she wished he would soon finish in the bathroom so she could shower. A hand to her head confirmed that unless there was some excellent conditioner supplied by the hotel, she'd remain in tangled disarray. That big hand seizing her hair, holding her helpless against that mind-blowing kiss—she scrubbed her knuckles over her lips in an attempt to erase the senses the memory evoked.

Easing from the bed, she scanned for her clothes and found them—in pieces, scattered about the room. Lord, and she hadn't even resisted the destruction of her favorite, comfy jeans. Not even a little. She'd been too busy anticipating—and demanding—the press of his body to hers. Her cheeks flushed with humiliation.

Crossing to her suitcase, she zipped it open and found her basic toiletries, some clean underwear and an outfit she hoped would be comfortable for the remainder of the trip. The discomfort of her apex would hopefully pass soon. Other females had sex on a regular basis and weren't bothered, but then they hadn't been pounded by an alpha with a huge—

She shut her thoughts down and stared grimly at the door. In several hours they'd be in his territory and she had no idea what—or who—awaited her there. Weren't mates supposed to learn about the other before they did the deed?

She wanted to rail against her fate. She'd come so close to getting away... She was also really tired, and yet her hormones weren't getting the message. Her wolf knew its mate was in the next room and it was beginning to clamor for more of the same treatment it had experienced just a couple of hours earlier. River hated herself in that moment, even more than she hated Jett.

It occurred that he hadn't punished her for breaking pack law, and she hoped he might forget. Ah, denial and rivers. That man was exactly the type who kept his promises. But there was no use thinking about it. She did reflect it was curious that there even had to be a pack law against the use of supplements to deter a claim. If being claimed was a she-wolf's destiny, why was there a way to circumvent it, and why were deterrents necessary? River had researched long and hard to find

them, but it stood to reason she wasn't alone.
There *were* women who chose not to be claimed and
took steps to protect against it. She'd been unlucky to
face such a potent male, and it was damn unfair no
matter how handsome—and virile—he was.

"Would you like to shower?"

She swallowed a tiny shriek and held her clothes
against her. Jett had exited the bathroom while she'd
been cogitating and she hadn't even heard him. Stupid
wolf self. Hard of hearing because she was thinking with
another body part.

His heated stare ignited her core and she
struggled to form a single word as intense need washed
over her. *No.* Managing a nod, she skirted his tall body,
clad only in a low-slung towel, and scurried into the
bathroom. She shut the door tightly and turned the latch,
though the flimsy knob wouldn't keep out a determined
wolf. Especially the aroused—if amused—one in the
next room.

Taking several deep breaths, she exerted her will
over her wolf and won the struggle for now. She moved
to the vanity. The disheveled woman reflected back from
the mirror didn't look at all familiar. Flushed and … well
used came to mind, and with it, her throat closed up. She
peered at his mating mark, turning her head this way and
that. There wasn't an obvious tear in the skin, merely a
slightly raised ridge, so he'd taken care with her, but
there was no doubt she was now a mated female. Jett's
mated female.

Swallowing another sob, she used the toilet,
wincing at the tenderness, and climbed into the shower.
She took a minute to use the steam option, hoping it
would release the simmering pheromones infused into
her skin by the alpha in the next room.

All the feminine necessities were lined up neatly

on the shelf and she buried her thoughts in the mundane process of washing and conditioning her hair. Scouring her body quickly, she used the little razor and rinsed off. She could sense Jett's impatience clear through the door, which had to be fanciful, but she remembered his worry about leaving his territory alone too long. The last thing she wanted was for him to see her as a burden and turn his ire her way.

Toweling off, she ran a comb through her hair to deal with any remaining tangles and pulled her clothes on, despite her skin being damp. Scrubbing her teeth, she then gathered up her toiletries and squared her shoulders before opening the door. To her surprise, the room was empty, a single paper cup of what looked to be coffee set on the table by the window. She sniffed and followed her nose. Coffee was vastly important in the broader scheme of life and she grabbed for it.

The strong, black flavor soothed her as it flowed over her tongue and down her throat. Maybe Jett had left her here, another fanciful thought, because his duffel was stacked beside her case. She set the container down and stuffed her little makeup kit away. There was no overt sign of her shredded clothing from yesterday, so there was nothing else to do but wait and finish the brew.

Why are you avoiding the issue, River? Quit skirting around and face up to it. You're stuck now. He's marked you—us. She didn't cast a wild glance around the room like the heroines in her romance novels did when they thought they were losing their minds and hearing voices. She knew exactly who was speaking to her. Her wolf was thrilled to be mated and was making no bones about it while looking forward to more … mating. With a sigh, she sipped at her coffee and hoped she and Jett could at least do some communicating of the verbal kind during the remainder of the drive. Her wolf settled, though River couldn't help but wonder if there wasn't some way of cutting loose…

The door clicked open and she turned on her heel to face him, taking care not to spill the last dregs of the bitter nectar.

"I hoped you took it black. I do, and I forget others might want cream or sugar."

"It's fine. Thank you." And wasn't she the prim little miss, considering all that had transpired between them?

"How are you?" His eyes conveyed real concern.

"Fine." She didn't want his concern.

He closed the gap between them with two long steps and she somehow managed not to retreat. A thrum set to playing in her core and she clenched the coffee cup with both hands so as not to lay one on him. Her first heat might have stolen all decorum and forced her to give over with abandon, but surely she could maintain an inkling of sanity before round two.

She flinched when his big hand came up and took hold of her jaw, turning it slightly to the right. He lifted her hair to one side and leaned so close she could individualize the notes of his soap and whatever scent he wore—unless it was pure male she was smelling. She closed her eyes in self-defense, so as not to stare at the roughhewn jaw directly in front of them.

"You've healed well." Male satisfaction laced his tone, and she knew it wasn't merely because his mark had closed up so nicely. Anyone who knew where to look would know she'd been claimed, and any wolf with half a nose would recognize who had done the claiming. A near hysterical giggle bubbled in the base of her throat as she thought about those dominance and submission books where one of them wore a collar. She supposed she should be grateful for a slight scar from a bite—no wolf would wear a collar.

"Are we leaving soon?" She was so relieved when he stepped back, taking the bulk of that tantalizing scent with him, that she wobbled.

Catching her arm, he steadied her. "Soon. I just checked us out but we have a little time. Are you able to manage your heat, River? Do I need to—"

"No! I'm fine. I thought you wanted to get back to your territory." She gingerly tugged her arm free, the imprint of his fingers as tangible as any brand. She so wasn't fine.

"Your well-being comes first."

"I'm *fine*."

With an exasperated huff, he paced to their cases. "I have a mother and two sisters, River. *Fine* is a word that doesn't accurately describe how you are feeling, but if you're sure…"

"I don't want to … to mate again." She shivered inwardly when he faced her and his chiseled mouth set in a hard line. Could he tell she was lying through her teeth?

"We *are* mated, River. If it's sex you're talking about, there will be a lot of that in our future. As you well know. Your heat will crest again soon and last a minimum of a week, maybe longer, unless you conceive you'll need to be sated. And then there are all the times in between the next one. Wolves don't go without. *I* don't go without."

Unable to contain the shiver that now permeated her entire body, she fought the nausea his words called up, all desire tamped. *She'd* gone without and it hadn't killed her or anything. But now she was destined for regular… Visions of being passed around to the single males of his pack danced in a horrid procession across her retinas and she swallowed hard to avoid spewing the coffee.

Her feet backed up of their own accord. "I won't let you. There must be some way to avoid that." She snarled her resolve at him and shock etched his features.

"River. You're my mate. It's part of what takes place between a mated pair."

"And anything else that suits you." The paper cup finally crumpled, no match for her burgeoning anger and anxiety. There wasn't much liquid left to spill, and it wasn't really hot any longer, but the remainder wet her hands and splashed her shirt.

Jett simply stared, as if trying to get inside her head. "River—" His phone signaled and his gaze dropped to the screen. "I need to take this."

She stormed to the bathroom and threw the container into the trash, rinsing her hands before mopping ineffectually at the stain. Tears coursed, unbidden, down her face and she grabbed a hand towel to soak them up. She'd be damned before she'd allow him to use her—or make her cry, though in truth she didn't exactly know how she'd get around it.

"We need to leave shortly," he called, and she knew better to resist. That implacable note was back, leaving her no doubt who was in charge. Her belly chose that moment to flare in concert with the heat in her core, and she groaned under her breath. The wolf was wide awake and pleading for release, unable to reconcile River's working brain's antipathy. Being in such close quarters was going to be excruciating.

She plodded out to join him, aware she was a sad disaster beside his effortless good looks and cared less. She avoided looking in even his general direction, though knew exactly where he was as if joined by an invisible thread. Her wolf preened and rolled over submissively and River wanted to run screaming.

The legs of the chair from the desk came into view. It was placed in the only vacant space in the room, and she stumbled to a stop. Her stare flew to him. Jett's visage was grim, his body tense beside it.

"What? Aren't we leaving?"

"I know you're waiting for the other shoe to drop, and I don't want to you think about it any longer than necessary. I also have an important meeting the minute I get home and don't want to delay your punishment further or spoil your first impression of your new home."

She shuffled sideways toward the door. "You won't spoil it. Maybe you don't have to do it at all. No one's the wiser and it's not like the supplements worked."

"River. Come here and get it over with."

"What are you going to do?" She risked a quick glance around, taking her eyes off him for a split second. His belt was still wrapped around his narrow hips, and there was no flogger in sight. She nearly laughed. Why would a visiting alpha require such a thing that he'd carry it with him? Unless he was a pervert.

"I'm going to paddle your ass. Did you think I'd beat you?"

"Your father would have, or ordered it done. In public."

"Traditionally, I suppose it would go like that in my—our—pack, if a female flouted convention like you did. But I'm not about to let my people know what you tried to pull. I didn't know you until last night, in any event, so I can't take it as a personal insult."

"Then can't you let it go? I didn't do it to personally reject you, right?"

His eyes danced with a light she figured was amusement, but his features remained set in a stern configuration. "It's happening, River. You need to make amends and it won't come between us again. So, get your sweet ass over here now, or I'll come get you. You can be uncomfortable sitting for a short while, or a long one."

Ah, now he was giving her choices. As if either was palatable. *Jerk.* She growled under her breath and glared, but marched over.

Jett dropped onto the chair. "Pants and underwear to your knees."

Humiliation stung her cheeks even as her core clenched. Her perverted wolf thought getting her ass paddled sounded like fun. With numb fingers she dealt with the button and zipper on her khakis and shoved them down, folding her plain panties out of sight inside the waistband. Her top covered her to the tops of her thighs, but that was somehow worse than nothing at all.

"Over my lap."

She took a few tiny, shuffling steps closer and awkwardly leaned forward. Feeling off balance lasted but a second as Jett caught her and lowered her into position. Her nose seemed to skim perilously close to the carpet and she automatically set her hands down. Her legs were imprisoned between his and cool air washed over her buttocks and thighs. Tears pricked and she scrunched her face behind the curtain of damp hair.

"Keep your hands out of the way and stay in position. You're getting twenty smacks and the intensity depends on how you receive them."

Like there was a protocol for this. Or maybe there was and she didn't get the memo. She mumbled what hopefully passed for understanding when she was really sending him a big *fuck you, Charlie.*

With no warning, a large hand descended across the fullness of her ass. The resounding crack probably made it sound worse than it felt, but both her ears and her tender skin were assaulted and she jerked. His other hand was promptly set in the small of her back and his strength immobilized her for the next whack.

Heat blossomed in its wake, and she wasn't thinking about her mating heat either—small mercy—because the punishing smacks following in a flurry weren't at all the sexual discomfort she'd been experiencing. They freaking hurt!

He covered her buttocks thoroughly and she lost count, though surely he'd soon be finished. Only one whimper escaped her tight throat and set lips, but there was nothing she could do about the tears that sprang free. An upswing slap to the base of her cheeks and one to the top of each thigh made her jerk and want to scream, and then it was over.

Jett swept her up and turned her to stand between his spread knees, his big hands grasping her waist. He stared into her eyes and she managed to meet his gaze despite the tears blurring her vision.

"All done, sweetheart. And you lived through it." He pulled her in for a hug and the solid bar of his cock pressed against her belly.

She wanted the contact and reassurance, as bizarre as that probably was, but the evidence of his arousal short-circuited something in her head. Shoving away from him, though still constrained by his hands, she made the accusation. "That turned you on!"

A smirk lifted a corner of his mouth and he didn't even try to dissuade her. "Having a beautiful woman squirming over my lap, against my cock, with her superior ass heating and turning pink under my palm... What can I say?"

"You're..." She couldn't come up with something nasty enough to describe him. Especially if he took exception and spanked her again.

"I'm what, sweetheart? I'm within my rights? I'm

a good guy for administering a fair and just punishment?"

She bit her bottom lip and bent to yank up her clothes. Jett brushed her hands out of the way and fastened her pants, the zipper purring loudly in her ears.

"Over and done, sweetheart. Know that I'll never punish you in anger and I won't harm you."

Did he think those were love taps? She surreptitiously slipped a hand behind her to touch a buttock. Of course, Jett noticed.

"You'll feel it for a bit," he conceded, "but nothing long lasting. And River? There's a huge difference between a punishment spanking and an erotic one."

"Well, I don't want another—of either type."

"I won't hold you to that."

She gritted her teeth and pulled away from him. Never again. She supposed the punishment worked, though, if she was already intent on not committing another punishable offense. But she couldn't leave it alone. "If you hit me again you'll wish you hadn't."

"Can you back up that threat, sweetheart?" His tone was silky, but she heard the annoyance beneath.

"I keep my promises, too, Jett."

He was quiet so long that she checked his face. He was watching her with that measured look she'd seen the first time they'd met as if to read her deepest thoughts. "Need the bathroom before we go? You might want to wash your face?"

It was obvious he picked his battles and had chosen to let that one go. A chill cooled her fury, seeing as he was in charge of who won the war.

"Nope. I'm good." Let that beauty on the desk see what the man she'd ogled a few hours ago was capable of. River was past being humiliated.

"Suit yourself. Just know that pouting is a bad look on you."

"Bully."

"What was that?"

"Nothing."

They made their way to the SUV and she climbed into the passenger seat without another word, snapping on her seat belt, resigned to a long and painful drive. Not to mention that the spanking had titillated her wolf and she'd likely paw him in her need or even worse. River would blame everything on her inner self from here on in. Pouting indeed. She didn't pout. And that beautiful brunette's jaw had dropped to the floor when she'd taken in the sight of the two of them. No doubt River's puffy face and swollen eyes, not to mention the limp she affected as she passed the receptionist had made an impression. The other woman didn't know how lucky she was.

Jett shut her door and then took his own place. He felt *grim* to her if there was such a feeling, and she cast her mind elsewhere, not interested in assessing his mood.

Once they were driving back on the interstate, he opened the conversation. "Tell me what you foresee in our relationship."

"I told you."

"Humor me. Repeat and expand on your viewpoint."

"I don't want to talk to you. You have all the power. I get that—didn't you just make that clear?"

"I enforce pack law, River. You're not immune. No one is. Not even me." He was pissed. She could hear it in his voice. Risking a glance in his direction, she saw how tightly he gripped the wheel and understood he was also struggling with control. What if they both lost it? Terror made her weak.

Carefully, she laid out what she believed her lot to be. "Now that you've claimed me, I belong to you. I answer to you. You'll expect obedience no matter what you ask of me. I'll have to give you as many children as you desire."

"Pretty sweeping statements there, River. What of the other things in your life? I thought you were an accountant."

Again, he surprised her. But she wasn't going to put much stock in his words. He hadn't said anything specific to challenge her other beliefs. "I am. I didn't think you'd let me work."

"I need someone with financial acuity. Who better than my ... obedient mate?"

Was he *teasing* her? She made herself look at him in an attempt to read him better. He glanced over and she recognized both humor and sincerity. If she could continue with her career, maybe there would be a modicum of freedom ahead. "I could do that."

"Then you're hired. The pay won't be great, but we'll probably save a ton of money. To help raise the twelve kids I want."

Twelve? An involuntary shudder overtook her, and she knew she appeared horrified. Jett laughed and shook his head. "We'll discuss how many kids, River. And I won't allow you to overtax your body in the event *you* want some huge number."

She hadn't thought about having kids, though she liked them. Determined not to mate, being a mother hadn't figured into her calculations. Perversely, she reflected that she wouldn't even be able to dictate a number, considering bossy Jett.

They rode in silence for a bit while she processed and he thought about whatever an alpha male thought about. All the while her need simmered and roiled, barely manageable, making her ache in personal places and her mouth dry.

"I hope to earn your respect and your trust." She jumped at the sound of his deep voice. "Someone has obviously twisted your perception of mates, and I'd like you to talk to me about that."

As if she could betray her mother's memory that way! The thought was like a bucket of cold water poured over her heat. "I don't know if I'll ever be able to trust you," she admitted, though somehow knew that was a harsh blow for Jett. He didn't respond, aside from a certain tension of his big body, and she hurried to continue. "It'll be hard to trust someone who took me away from my home, thwarted my plan for independence, and mated me. Even when you knew I was dead set against it. " And then there was the punishment. Oh, she'd earned it, but refused to see it as making amends. *Because you rejected his forgiveness.* Of course, she had. She hated the paternalistic bent of shifter life.

"I hope we can get past that. In time. Because I believe we are fated mates and all your planning—and mine—has gone by the wayside."

Fated? That didn't happen. Except rarely. She shook her head. Maybe in folklore.

Jett pointed out, "You're in my mind already, and I'm in yours to some degree. You're feeling my moods intensely although we hardly know one another. That kind of connection usually takes time to develop."

He wasn't wrong, and it scared the shit out of her. How was she going to keep any part of her separate from him? He'd absorb her like her father did her mother and she'd fall over herself trying to please him. She'd do anything he said, anything he wanted...

"River! Stop torturing yourself and talk to me!"

"I don't know what you want me to say!"

"What is it you fear the most, being mated?" He posed the question in a calm, supportive tone, and it diffused her angst a trifle.

"Being forced to do whatever you tell me."

Jett made a strange choking sound, and she felt the vehicle lean to the right. She glanced out the window and realized he was pulling over. He came to a stop and shut the engine down. It ticked over as he focused on her in the relative silence. Residual surprise and concern softened his craggy features.

She had a sudden urge to kiss him, to touch him, and knew she telegraphed it by the way his eyes flared and darkened. She wrapped her arms around her chest instead and hugged them tight. Stupid, horny wolf.

He said, "You don't know me, I get that. You don't know that I say what I mean and mean what I say."

"I think you're honorable," she blurted. "I feel that you are." Although why she'd think that when he'd spanked her...

He smiled and her fingers twitched. "Honor is important to me, sweetheart. And I won't force you to do anything."

"But I'll want to please you. You said that. And I know what that means."

"You *will* want to please me. As I'll want to please you. But you won't have to do anything you object strongly to. I can't think of anything, off the top of my head that you'd find objectionable."

"I object to you hitting me."

"Then follow pack rules."

"You might want to sleep with one eye open," she muttered, although she'd never acted out physically, and in truth had no idea how she might back up that threat.

"If you promise violence, I can see I might have to tie you to my bed."

The air in the vehicle thickened at his suggestive reply and she couldn't fill her lungs. Being restrained, despite already being at this man's mercy, was a terrifying thought and even her wolf backed up at her reaction.

"Damn it, River. What the fuck?" He fit his hand around her chin and lifted her face, staring into her.

Finally breathing through her response, she searched the pale blue of his eyes, and saw only concern and worry. "You scared me."

"I see that. I wasn't being literal."

"Okay." He stroked her hair and despite her reluctance, she allowed herself the comfort—this time.

"Can you tell me anything else that you'd object to? Help me out here, sweetheart. I'm not a mind reader."

"What about sex?"

He slowly took his hand away, and she very nearly leaned after it. Or her wolf did. "Does it really come down to that, River? Did you find our coupling so abhorrent?"

"I haven't thought about it." She would have called the words back if she could. What male would take such a blow to his pride as to hear his sexual skills so forgettable? That might be breaking pack law as well. Her buttocks drew up.

Jett burst into laughter. Her ears rang with the sound and she nearly joined him. Her wolf pressed hard and suggested joining him in other ways.

"You crush me yet again, sweetheart. I, personally, can't stop remembering how you surrendered. How lovely your body is and how hot and slick you became. You took me fully, despite your inexperience."

She wasn't laughing now. Embarrassment flushed her cheeks. "I expect the mating heat allowed for that," she mumbled.

Not deterred, Jett continued to chuckle. "Your first heat no doubt was helpful," he said agreeably, "but I have room for comparison, and our first time was memorable."

And now he was bragging, the jerk. "How nice for you then, that you've honed your craft," she replied, with transparent saccharine sweetness. "But like I said, I haven't really thought about it."

"You are really the most obstinate female. So strong willed. I couldn't have chosen better. I look forward to the challenge."

"Of what? Breaking me to your will?"

All semblance of humor vanished, and Jett looked as forbidding as she'd ever seen him. "I won't need to break you, River. I won't need to restrain you or otherwise scare you. In time you'll see the truth of our connection for yourself."

She bit her lip and turned away, staring out the windshield while her wolf whined about lost opportunities and disparaged her fears as nonsensical. But the animal wouldn't care who she fucked, who her mate was, as long as her needs were met and her heat addressed. The knowledge was sobering and River resolved to shore up her control in any way possible.

"I need to get home. My council will be waiting. You think on things and we'll talk later." Jett pulled back into traffic and brought the SUV up to speed. It was clear she'd truly insulted him this time, and if she was honest, he didn't know the specifics of what he was up against.

She railed inwardly, having missed an opportunity to tell him those specifics, a tiny hope flickering that he wouldn't make her have sex with others. Soon they'd be on his turf and he was angry—or disappointed—in her, so broaching the subject would be even harder. What if things unraveled before they could talk? Because she had to state her case and maybe get him to promise not to pass her around. As Alpha, perhaps he could get away with it.

"Jett?"

"Not now, River. I need to have my head clear and straight for the meeting. You turn me upside down with your convoluted thinking, and I have to focus. I'll take you to my home and we'll talk after the meeting."

"Sure." She shifted on the seat, pressing her thighs together and tried for more math equations and problems, losing the battle against her rising heat. Stupid call of nature.

"I'll help you with that before long."

Did he know those smug, oh-so-male remarks fueled her fury and distracted from the sexual desperation? Another thing she didn't want to give him credit for.

Chapter Four

He might tear his hair out. Not even a full day in his female's company and he was being driven insane. Okay, that was overstating it. But he'd told the utter truth when he called her obstinate and strong willed. Maybe not compliments many females would aspire to, yet he felt a certain admiration. But River was determined to paint him with the same brush as other males she obviously detested and was reluctant to cut him any slack.

And then there was her simmering need. As he'd feared, the hurried claiming hadn't assuaged it to any depth, and the push-pull of nature was going to fuel her deepest fears.

Administering her punishment was necessary—and convenient in the short term. He didn't want her worrying about it any longer, and he figured the spanking had both canceled any obligatory feelings she might be experiencing as well as briefly tamping down her heat. What concerned him was her refusal to be cosseted afterward, let alone the fear that permeated her being.

It wasn't an ideal time to take a mate, and he'd nearly refused his sire and rescheduled for the future. But if he had, he never would have met River. So the timing was fated.

However, he had to focus on the pack for the time being. Tahl, his first lieutenant, had been the one to place the call earlier and update him. Two rogues had made incursions on one of his businesses and while easily repelled, it spoke to a probing action. There were likely others waiting to see how Jett responded.

He had to meet with his council and firm up a plan, one of many constructed in preparation for situations like this. And he had to set the issue with River aside so he could do his job as Alpha, although she was also part of his job. Duty and mating could go hand in hand, but he wanted them to be separate. He had yet to get to the bottom of her antipathy. His head hurt with everything he was trying to process.

Blue Star, his town—nearly a city—sprawled in the distance and he heaved a sigh of relief. Within minutes he was pulling up to the large log cabin on the outskirts that was his home and also served as the meeting place for his council. Several trucks and one muscle car—Tahl's—were parked haphazardly in the yard, and he caught a glimpse of a silhouette in the big front window.

"We're here."

"You have a nice home. Large. Roomy." River sounded like a real estate agent, except for the worry and fear undermining the compliment.

"It works. My mother and sisters helped me decorate, but you can change anything you like. The yard too. There's a pool out back and a big deck for entertaining."

"I'm sure it's fine. Nice."

When he paddled her for the supplement issue, he should have added a few whacks to address her facile use of *fine*. Well, there would likely be another time. He suspected she hadn't given up the idea of running and that was something he couldn't tolerate one iota. Not when it meant her safety would be in jeopardy. "Come inside. I won't take the time today to introduce you other than to announce you as my mate, but you'll have to meet the council members in due course. But I have business—"

"Sure. Of course. No hurry. Business comes first." River fell over herself to accommodate him and he wondered why before brushing it aside. She was out of the vehicle and standing beside it before he could disembark. He observed her making fists and staring around.

"Nothing to worry about, sweetheart." He tugged her fingers apart and took a hand, pulling her along to the entrance.

Tahl opened one of the big double doors as they climbed the steps, and River shrank. Jett *felt* her lose stature. He tightened his grip, supposing the other male was an imposing figure if a very handsome one to judge by the females who fawned over him. "This is Tahl, my first lieutenant. He's like a brother to me and you'll get to know him well."

She quaked and the scent of terror again rocked him. Tahl noticed too, one blond eyebrow quirking upward as he sent Jett a questioning glance.

"Tahl, my mate, River Fortuna from the Mystic River pack. My father's pack," he clarified, though Tahl knew exactly what he was talking about while doubtlessly wondering what had set River off.

"River. Congratulations, Jett. I look forward to getting to know your mate." His lieutenant inclined his head and obviously thought better of offering to shake.

River made a squeaking sound that might have passed for a hello, and Jett motioned Tahl away with a tiny shake of his head. What the fuck? He dropped her hand and slipped his arm around her waist, drawing her to the stairs. "Our room is this way."

She leaned into him for support and crept up the stairs, though he would have carried her if not for wanting to give her as much control as possible. Opening the door, he walked her inside. "The bathroom is there. You can rest if you like. If you're hungry, the kitchen—"

"I'm not hungry. I'm fine. I think … Tahl and

your council are waiting, right? I'll just stay here. In your room."

"I'll have someone bring your case up so you can unpack."

"It's okay. I can wait. Unless they want to leave it in the hall? In case I'm in the bathroom or something."

Torn, he glanced toward the door and back at River. Instinct told him to stay and deal with her, and find out why she was afraid to even meet someone delivering her luggage. But so much time had passed and his council was waiting. "I'll be back as soon as we're finished. Would you rather wait to meet the council members until a later date?"

"Yes! Sure. That works."

He hauled her to him and was relieved when her initial tension ebbed and she nearly relaxed against him, one small hand clutching his shirt. Rubbing her back seemed to ease her a little bit more. He pressed a kiss on her hair. "See you soon, sweetheart."

He shut the door firmly behind him, his last look of her a waif-like figure worrying her bottom lip between her teeth. His wolf surged and demanded that he protect her, and he warred with the animal until hearing the lock catch softly. Shoving his concern and the mystery of River's behavior to the back of his mind, knowing she was safe, he headed into the gathering room where his council waited. To a man, they stood, and a fleeting thought of a female like River taking a seat on council flickered in his brain before Tahl advanced to meet him.

"Your mate?" His lieutenant knew better than to mention anything about River's reaction where all ears could hear, so posed it like a polite query. If the other members needed to know, if it should affect the pack, Jett would share later.

"Upstairs, resting."

"Her heat is…"

"Not yet sated. I know, Tahl. And I curse the timing. Let's get this done so I can tend to her."

Rees and Davis lounged into their seats once he took his, and Rick followed suit. Only Kris hesitated. The tall wolf said, "You are mated. And she's here."

He'd never liked Kris, but the male had mad strategy skills like he could climb into the enemy's head. Jett chose all his council, after his father's six had returned to their pack, and he hadn't picked them for friendship. "I am. To one of my father's pack. You'll meet her another time."

Kris smiled, but it rubbed Jett the wrong way. The council member said, "She's still in heat."

"She is."

"Will you share her?"

Not in this fucking lifetime. Jett pulled himself together. He alone would meet River's needs. He hoped. "If that's what she requires."

Tahl cleared his throat and Kris dropped the subject, giving Jett a nod. He tamped down his desire to rip the other man's throat out and called the meeting to order.

They discussed the incursion and the results of the interrogation of the surviving wolf. Interestingly enough, that rogue caved immediately upon being offered a place in the pack once—if—he proved trustworthy. He'd shared that the rogues were loosely connected, led by a hard individual referred to as the Regent.

The male apparently ruled through brute force and terror, and only those who saw violence as a calling and craved what the Regent could offer were part of his pack. Jett's newest member—should he accept him—had wanted out for some time, his stomach turned by what he'd seen and been forced to participate in, and had leaped at the opportunity to invade Jett's territory and perhaps escape. That explained how easily he was captured. Jett reserved judgment until he met the man, but Rees believed he had the straight goods.

Rees had also thought to inquire about females and the word that the rogues helped themselves to other packs' women silenced the room. There had been rumors circulating from packs further west that young, single females had dropped out of sight, and no one had been able to locate them. There wasn't a male present who didn't appreciate the opposite sex and fucking ranked high on the list of down-time activities. And sometimes surpassed duty, though Davis had reined things in of late. A confrontation by his Alpha had that effect.

But the thought of female wolves being at the mercy of rogues... Jett knew his disgust and rage was mirrored by his council. He'd weeded out those in the pack who would abuse others, especially females and children, and knew the more progressive packs did the same thing. He froze for a moment. Was his father's pack progressive? Involuntarily, his head tilted back and he stared up at the ceiling as if he could see into the room where River waited. What had happened?

"What's your recommendation, Jett?" Kris no doubt had all the strategic plans in his head.

"You're sure this male is giving you accurate information?"

Rees nodded. "The important pieces, anyhow. I confirmed it with other sources."

"Then we'll take the fight to them. Find the Regent and take care of him personally. The rest will scatter and can be dealt with fairly easily."

Tahl nodded. "There will be inevitable difficulties from the ones who survive, 'cause it's unlikely we'll get them all, and it's the price of having rogues. But like you said, they'll scatter and one rogue at a time is manageable. What about the females?"

Jett's mind flashed to the thought of female rogues, though he knew that wasn't what Tahl was asking. River would have been considered rogue, had she been successful in running, and at some point would have been hunted down and either returned to her pack or terminated. Humans and wolves had lived amicably for decades, but only because pack law ensured safety. Yet she had chosen to go rogue regardless.

He shook his head and answered his lieutenant. "We'll bring them back here and tend to them."

"Your mate will have her hands full, Jett. It'll be a tough introduction to our pack." Rees reminded him of River's expected role as his mate.

"She's up to the task." And he believed she was, or would be. "Get the word out and put some teams together. We need to act on the info before they figure out we might know where they're at and move operations. Let me know when you're ready."

Tahl shoved his chair back. "Consider it done. You'll have a couple of hours."

Time to ease River's heat again, and he scoffed at it sounding like a hardship. She was likely suffering, albeit in silence. He got up and strode from the room, certain in the knowledge that he'd made the right decision and his council would carry out the plan.

His duffel and her large suitcase sat outside the bedroom door. Tahl was a great multitasker and had arranged for someone to haul them up. Jett rapped on a panel and there was a brief wait before the lock disengaged and River swung it wide. Hectic color painted her cheeks and she trembled like a leaf in a gale. He swept her up and held her closely.

"You're okay. It's only me."

"I know," she mumbled. "I know your step."

"Are you still frightened? Will you tell me what scares you?"

She shook her head, and her hair brushed over his bicep. "I'm okay."

He didn't scent fear so much as need, but this time, he wanted her to ask. "What do you want, River?"

A quiet moan vibrated against his chest and her breath huffed warmly, right through his shirt. She nestled closer and her soft belly teased his cock.

"River?"

"I need you." He'd take those three words, though they were grudgingly offered through gritted teeth and spoken so quietly only a wolf would hear.

"Take your clothes off. I already owe you an outfit."

She stepped back, and he reluctantly let her go, heartened to see a ghost of a smile lift the corners of her full lips at the mention of her other clothes, even as her hands faltered in the attempt to seize the hem of her shirt.

He stripped off his own and reveled in the wide-eyed look she gave his chest. Never giving much thought to his physique—shifters were generally well built and he trained with Tahl every day—he nonetheless was pleased she liked what she saw. A look of concern replaced that look, however, when he stepped out of his jeans, having gone commando.

"It fits fine, sweetheart."

She glared. "Are you killing the mood on purpose? Trying to embarrass me?"

Knowing a chuckle would really piss her off, he helped her pull her top over her head, giving him a moment to straighten his face. "Don't ever lose that sweet innocence, River."

"I'd say that ship sailed earlier today," she retorted, as he popped the catch on her bra. It slipped down her arms, the cups snagging on her beaded nipples, and his cock jumped in response to the sight. "No one would call me innocent now."

"There are many different forms, sweetheart." He crouched to work her pants down her legs, taking a pair of basic cotton underwear with them. His sister would have to take her shopping, though he'd buy her lingerie. Catching her by the thighs, he buried his face in her sex before she could step out of the tangle of fabric. Her scent made his temples pound and her taste... Tart honey met his questing tongue.

"Jett! What are you...? You can't..." A flailing hand grabbed at his hair.

Her thighs parted instinctively and he pressed the advantage, supporting her with a hand under her sweet ass and the other at her waist. River bowed back over it, giving him full access, and she quickened with but a few well-placed licks followed by suction over her clit. Both of her hands tightened to tug hard at his scalp.

She screamed something indecipherable as he drove her up again, his tongue high in her channel before once more tormenting that tiny bundle of nerves at her apex. When she was a trembling mass, he rose, face drenched with the evidence of a satisfied female, and carried her to his bed.

One handed, he dragged the covers back and nearly dropped her to the mattress on her belly. "Hands and knees, sweetheart." He nearly growled the command and the wolf in her responded, because River was lax, sprawled bonelessly after two momentous orgasms.

He shoved a pillow beneath her belly and pushed her thighs wide, her fine buttocks rounding with the movement. There was no sign of his spanking and he wished for even a slight palm print to press his lips against. The swollen lips of her pussy were framed enticingly, and he noted her tiny puckered star. She'd be a virgin there too and he couldn't wait to introduce her to the pleasure of anal sex. *Will you share her?* Kris's question intruded and Jett's gut clenched. Females enjoyed threesomes and some demanded them—and more—if their heat wasn't eased. Unleashing a female's sexuality meant fulfilling all their fantasies.

Locking that unpalatable thought down, he focused on the immediate, and that was quenching his mate's heat, especially as he'd be joining a team in a matter of hours. River hitched on the pillow, her head dropping lower, and he admired the stance of her wolf.

Grasping his shaft, he notched it at her opening and teased inward past the initial stricture to be held tightly by the engorged walls of her pussy. He groaned at the indescribable sensation of liquid heat and River moaned in response, pushing into him.

On his knees, he held her steady and saw to his own pleasure. Lost in the joy of fucking his mate, he soon powered to climax, emptying his balls until they cramped, with River acquiescent beneath him.

His cock didn't soften, and he didn't merely slip free of her, having to pull out against clenching tightness. He wanted to go again, maybe after she sucked him to the edge. Or she could ride him—he could visualize those full breasts bouncing with their tips pointed high and hard. He hadn't kissed her nearly enough either. But they were out of time.

Collapsing at her side, his cock painting a wet line over one buttock, he drew his palm down her spine. "River?"

"Um?"

"I have to go."

She lifted her head a little and blinked through a curtain of that multi-colored hair. "What?"

"I have to go. Pack business."

Orgasmic bliss leached from her pretty face and she curled up as if to hide again. "How long will you be gone? I mean, will I stay here? Alone?"

"I don't know how long. But you won't be alone."

A pulse beat wildly at the base of her neck and he set a finger there to sooth it. "What's wrong?"

"Who will be with me?"

"I've asked my youngest sister to come. Desiree. My mother's away but should be home in a few days. And you'll have a guard."

"A guard?"

"Someone to ensure your safety. We've had some trouble, remember?" Not that he'd been specific. There was no point in worrying her about what he planned when she was already so tense.

"Right. I remember you mentioned it. So, your sister? She'll stay here?" Her throat seemed hoarse from screaming her orgasms.

"She will. She isn't mated. I called her this morning. You explore the house. Think on what I said about decorating and such. If you cook, do so. Order supplies in if you like. Treat this like your home, River, because it is. Okay?"

"Okay."

He knew she wouldn't think of changing anything, but had to hope. Desiree would be a good influence if River let her in. "Great. I'll be back as soon as I can, and I'll call you. I put my number in your phone and if you need me you call."

"Okay."

"How about I get you in the tub?" He shoved to

his feet and offered his hand.

"I can manage."

"I know you can, but I want to help. I want to take care of you, as I suspect it's been a long time since anyone has." She blinked, this time to hold the tears at bay to judge by the way her eyes glistened, and his chest ached. "C'mon, River. Get up. It's not like I haven't seen it all."

"Jerk." She said it under her breath, but her ire was apparent as she struggled off the bed, ignoring his hand. His little taunts worked every time, and in the future he hoped she'd take it for the gentle teasing it was.

Leading her into the attached bath, he opened the taps to let the water thunder into the enormous tub, adding a handful of salts. "I don't have any feminine bath stuff, but that's Epsom. I expect you're a little … tender."

Her blush began at the slope of her breasts and crept up her throat to flood her cheeks. Much like when she climaxed. He watched, fascinated, before realizing she was also clenching her fists. "Just making an observation, sweetheart. Claiming is, uh, vigorous."

"I noticed."

"So you were paying attention this time?"

"I paid attention last time. Sort of. I said that I hadn't given it much thought—afterward."

"Ouch. I deserved that." He grabbed her and swung her into the tub, enjoying her startled shriek. "Soak. I'm gonna take a quick shower and grab something to eat. I'll leave a plate for you in the fridge."

Nearly afloat in the deep tub, her hair wet around her shoulders, River stared up at him. Her limbs stretched in long, wavy lines beneath the water, the hair on her mound a mere smudge, and her round breasts bobbed enticingly. A combination of sweet and sultry siren, he could almost read the conflicted thoughts rolling around in her head. He *could* read the satiation of her body and figured he'd assuaged her heat well enough—at least until he returned. And then he'd come to discover all of her needs.

Thrusting away a certain darkness that lowered with that thought, he went to shower.

Chapter Five

Jett had hustled out of the bathroom right after cleaning up. He'd stopped to lean down and press a kiss on her lips but that was all. Not that she required anything else. She didn't even need that kiss or care to think about his superbly made body and what it was capable of. Thank goodness her wolf was still asleep or it would have riled her up and he might have made time to do her again.

She carefully washed between her thighs and winced. It was a really good thing he hadn't made the time. She didn't want to review what transpired in their second coupling, at least not in minute detail, but it was hard not to think about the way he'd brought her to orgasm. Or the way their bodies fit together. With a groan, she surged up and grabbed for a towel before dripping over to the shower to rinse off.

Standing in the rush of warm water, she felt curiously content and gave her state of mind—and body—some consideration. Her heat was assuaged for the moment certainly, but while the future remained uncertain, her fear had diminished. She should feel hollow, drained from the cacophony of emotions she'd experienced over the past twenty-four hours or so… It came to her. She and her wolf were no longer at odds. Now her inner self was no longer denied, she was almost relaxed for the first time in a very long time.

But then Jett had gone someplace after doing his duty with her, so this was a period of respite. She didn't put any stock in how … compatible they were, other than because of the claiming. That was nature. There was nothing more to it and she wasn't especially tuned to him nor him to her. She shut off the shower with a quick snap of the faucet and quit pondering.

His sister might be here by now and Lord knew she needed another female for company, even if it was Jett's relation who would probably think he walked on water. Without Cass around—and he hadn't said River could call her little sister yet—she'd pretty much take anyone. The more she learned about this pack and figured out her place in it, the better off she'd be. Best she didn't think about the downside and allow the familiar miasma of dread to threaten her relative calm.

What did one wear to meet the Alpha's family? She selected her best pair of jeans and a silky, short-sleeved top in a soft swirl of green and taupe. Putting her hair up in a high ponytail, she wiped on some mascara and lip gloss before stepping into a pair of flats.

Cautiously unlocking the door—had Jett locked it behind him to ensure her privacy or had he noticed her paranoia?—she pulled it open and glanced into the hall. No sign of anyone, but she thought she could hear voices emanating from downstairs. She moved quickly along the second floor, glancing into three bedrooms, all sporting queen-size beds and elegant furniture. A large central bathroom, nearly as nice as the one belonging to Jett, completed the visual tour. There were no locked rooms that might pique her curiosity, though she'd have a look around downstairs.

Taking the stairs, she stood at the bottom and realized the house branched off in different directions with the staircase being a central point. Dark hardwood floors ran through out with the exception of the tiled entry.

She poked her head into a large room furnished with an enormous wooden table and at least a dozen chairs and concluded it was a meeting area. The scent of several virile shifters still permeated the air and she hurriedly backed out, turning right to find an open living area leading into a good sized dining room. As with the second floor, everything was immaculate and the furniture and window coverings blended nicely. Not that she was any decorator, but it was pleasing to the eye. The kitchen must be across the way, and she followed the sound of conversation, picking out a male and female voice.

Squaring her shoulders, she advanced and found herself in an area worthy of a magazine spread, absolutely nothing like her kitchen at home. Chrome and stainless steel vied for a polished look and she thought the countertops were black granite. Gray cabinets stretched to the ceiling. She took it all in, in one awestruck sweep before the individuals occupying the space became silent and turned to stare.

"Hello." As far as awkward went, it ranked right up there. The tall, statuesque female had to be Jett's sister, with the same wintry eyes and ebony hair, only hers spilled down her back nearly to her hips. The male wolf hulked—there was no other way to describe him. Muscles bulked on muscles and made him look shorter than he probably was, and his bald pate was a surprise. Wolves were never hairless in human form, in her experience. She took a second to note that he had absolutely no interest in her and her relief made her light headed.

The female smiled widely, and it felt sincere, especially when she stepped forward and grabbed River's hands, squeezing them gently. "You'll be River! I'm Desiree. We knew Jett had gone to seek a mate, but he wasn't certain one would be suitable. But you are! And you're here!"

Compared to Desiree, who exuded supreme confidence, backed up by her gorgeous face and stunning body clad in an amazing royal blue dress and matching heels, River couldn't hope to measure up. Why was the other woman so happy to see her?

"I am. River, that is. And I'm here." *Oh, clever. Make her think you're a dullard too.*

Desiree didn't seem to notice, gesturing to the male. "This is Max. Fitting name, eh?" She giggled and it sounded like music. River laughed too and nodded at Max but kept her distance. One could never be too careful.

He nodded back and kept his. "Pleased to meet you. Jett left *me* here to keep watch. You and Desiree are to remain in the house with the doors and windows locked, the alarm on."

"Okay." Where had Jett gone and why did Max sound so annoyed that he'd been left? Jett had said business...

"Don't scare her," Desiree chided. "We'll hang out inside and behave, though the pool looks inviting. You do your guard thing."

The behemoth nodded again, naked scalp catching the overhead lighting, and ambled out of the room. Or maybe he was too big to amble. But he didn't make a sound. River watched him go and breathed a sigh of relief.

"You okay?"

"Sure. I..." She debated putting it out there, used to keeping secrets, but this young woman seemed pretty nice and her earlier thought of finding an ally and confidant surfaced. "I'm uncomfortable around male wolves is all."

Desiree nodded as if she understood. "Some of them warrant caution. Especially the rogues. And there are a few in our pack who can be disrespectful."

River couldn't help it. She

73

snorted. *Disrespectful.* Hardly what she meant.

"Excuse me?" If a woman could wrinkle her brow and look enticing, it was Desiree.

"Sorry. I was thinking beyond disrespectful."

"Like rogue behavior?"

"Is there a difference?"

Jett's sister gaped—looking gorgeous doing it. "I would hope there's a difference. Jeez, River. What goes on in your pack?"

Wishing she hadn't opened the conversation, River shrugged. "The usual."

"What's the usual? I mean, Jericho is Jett's sire and my brother hasn't said anything untoward about that pack. Maybe he doesn't know?"

"I didn't want to mate. But I had no choice."

"Sister, we need a drink for this discussion. C'mon, we'll find an expensive bottle of wine from Jett's cellar and have some girl talk."

She followed Desiree to a small room with a heavy door. The walls were lined with racks of wine, and the temperature was obviously controlled. A huge fridge held dozens of other bottles, evident through the glass doors.

"Red or white?"

"Red." She might not be as classy as Desiree but she knew a little about wines.

"Great. My preference too." The other female ran a manicured finger along a rack and plucked a bottle free. "This one's my favorite."

They opened it at the island and poured big goblets full, and then carried them into the living area. Desiree dropped down on the end of a leather couch, pulling one long leg up beneath her and pointed to the other end. River set her glass down on the heavy wooden coffee table before taking her seat.

"So spill. I don't think I've ever met a wolf who actually said she didn't want to mate. Not a male wolf either."

It was what Desiree inferred that caught River's attention. Taking a sip of the robust liquid first, she swallowed slowly in appreciation. "So while you haven't met one, you think there might be a few of us who don't want to mate?"

"I'm sure of it, though Jett would strangle me if I said it out loud."

River's spirits drooped and she drank more wine. So her mate really did believe it was destiny, not that it mattered now. What was done was done. *She'd* been done. "Uh huh. He's pretty adamant on the subject."

"It's more that he fears what will happen to those who leave the pack. You know, go rogue and end up in trouble, get tracked down and terminated. If they don't agree to return to the pack. Or a pack."

She hadn't eaten for a while, and the wine made her head buzz. Wolves metabolized spirits quickly, so it had to be her empty belly. Regardless, she was overwhelmed at the idea she could have been considered rogue. Only males went rogue, didn't they? "That's antiquated thinking."

Desiree considered her wine, peering into the glass. "I sometimes think so, except we've got a big problem right now with rogue wolves chipping away at different packs' territory. Max told me they are taking females and I doubt that bodes well."

River realized she needed to rethink some of her more recent choices. She still resented being claimed, particularly without even a rudimentary introduction, but it could have gone worse. And with a worse man. Her wolf purred at the thought of Jett and River clenched her thighs together. *Not now.*

Desiree was staring, a horrified look on her face. "Oh my gosh, River. How could I be so stupid?" She leaned over and snaffled the wine glass. "You're still in heat, so you probably aren't pregnant yet, but you need to be careful! Jett will kill me."

"Your brother seems to possess a violent streak." She couldn't help being snarky, embarrassed by both Desiree's observation and her own stupidity.

"Oh, he does, not that you'll ever see it." The young female set her own drink down. "I'll get us both something soft in a minute. But if you didn't want to be mated, how did you plan to avoid it?"

"By going rogue, not that I thought about it that way," she admitted.

"Wow. I can see we're blessed with the addition to our family. I bet you drive Jett insane. Good for you. I can't wait for you to meet Mom and Lizbeth. They're gonna love you."

"You think so?"

"For sure. You'll see. But that's later. Tell me what you think of my big brother."

"Um. He's okay."

Desiree threw herself back on the cushion and laughed. Loudly. "Faint praise," she choked. "You're killing me."

"I met him late afternoon yesterday, Desiree, and the next thing we were on the road to here. And I was claimed in between."

The other woman sobered and shook her head. "River, I'm sorry. Again. I tend to be self-absorbed and not always sensitive to others. You must be overwhelmed."

"I am." *And anxious, and scared. And starved.*

"But you're mated. He claimed you."

"True."

"So he must want you. I mean, there had to be an attraction."

"I guess I was suitable." No way was she copping to taking supplements. The next thing she'd be telling Desiree that her brother spanked women. Not that she'd ever see his violent streak—she hoped.

"You're not his usual type, and I'm not saying that to be a bitch. I know my brother, though, and you are more than suitable. Or you wouldn't be here, claimed."

"My Alpha, well, my old Alpha picked me for your brother," she explained, curious as to Jett's *type*. No, she wasn't. "You know, Jericho wanted a female from his pack to join with Jett and build bridges between the two packs. And because he's Jett's father." Though there were a number of other females back home to choose from.

"Uh uh. Jericho might have picked you as a candidate, but Jett doesn't march to his sire's drum. Nope, it was Jett's decision. And I can see why."

River desperately wanted to know why but wouldn't ask. "You keep referring to Jericho as *Jett's* father. Isn't he yours?"

"No."

Well, that was interesting. "Would it be okay for me to ask something? Like how my old Alpha has a son here and a mate and sons back home? I thought, you know, that we mated for life and had pups within that relationship."

Desiree's lovely face closed off. "That's true under normal circumstances. But my mother is anything but, same as her relationship with Jericho. It's complicated. And that's for Jett and Mom to explain."

"I'm in over my head."

"Politics are the same across packs, I expect. And you'll soon be acting as the Alpha's mate. If you struggle, I'll have your back and Jett won't expect you to be perfect. After all, you obviously have some pretty novel ideas and it remains to be seen how they will integrate."

River wasn't going to argue that fact. "Can we get some tea or something? I'm hungry too. It's been a long time since dinner yesterday." Not to mention she'd used a ton of calories. She had a mild headache too, denoting the definite possibility that the coffee today had been decaf. It stood to reason that Jett would be perfect in choosing that beverage for her, aware she might have conceived. She should feel humbled and grateful for his concern, but all she experienced was annoyance.

"Dinner! I am such an idiot. C'mon. Jett has all kinds of things prepared for him. We'll raid the fridge and failing that, the freezer. Max will want something too."

She wondered who prepared things for Jett and chewed on the inside of her cheek so she didn't ask that either. She was definitely taking an inordinate interest in her mate, even if a lot of what she thought was negative, and she wondered if she could blame it all on nature.

They found a large plate of cold cuts and cheese in the huge refrigerator, and there were crusty rolls in the pantry. Jett had kept that promise too.

"Do you cook?" Desiree sorted napkins.

"Yes. My mother died when I was ten, so I kinda took over. There's just me and my little sister and our father."

"That's hard, River. Our dad—Lizbeth's and mine—was killed repelling a rogue attack about five years ago. I miss him lots. My mom stayed single afterward, so she was hit hard too. You don't have a stepmother?"

She noted that Desiree's mother hadn't been

deterred by the absence of Jericho Reeves in taking a mate, but then they hadn't been mated. Except wolves didn't conceive unless they were a pair—she didn't think. Were there other things she didn't know? Hopefully, she'd have her curiosity satisfied sooner than later. "No. Maybe my dad felt the same as your mom."

"You don't know?"

"We've never talked about it. I was ten. And we aren't close." Strange that she would be feeling sad about that now, and missing her dad just a little.

"Sit at the island. Max will sniff out the food soon and join us, so get something on your plate before it's gone." Desiree winked.

They made their selections and River said, "You aren't mated."

"Not yet. I have my eye on someone but he's playing coy."

"Wait. *You* have your eye on someone? But you're a female." Definitely, things were different here.

"In this pack females tend to indicate our interest, and not just for casual sex."

"Okay. It doesn't work that way back home. I mean, casual sex is allowed, but the males chase. And the Alpha blesses the request to claim." Did this have something to do with Jett's mother's situation?

Max ghosted in and took a seat before she could think of a way to casually inquire. The platters magically emptied before River's fascinated eyes.

Desiree said, "We're a progressive pack. Just ask Max."

"Don't involve me in your female machinations, Desi." The big male spoke around a mouthful of food.

"I was explaining that females are allowed to express their inclination for a mate, past casual, rather than have Jett and the council arbitrate. Like you and

Josie did."

Max's face and scalp bloomed deep red and he stuffed another bite in his mouth.

River stared in between him and Desiree, and the young female explained, "Josie set her sights on Max a long time ago and he dodged her. But she was determined and when she came into her first heat, she contrived to be where he was. And the rest is history. Jett knew she was interested and also aware Max wasn't adverse, just shy."

"Damn it, woman. Can you not shoot your mouth off?"

"Aww Max, Josie's my best friend. You think I don't know everything that happened, every freaking step of the way? And it's not like River won't be privy to most everything that takes place in the pack."

River heard Max mutter something about hoping Desiree didn't know *everything.* She choked on a giggle and immediately apologized to the big man. She didn't find anything remotely humorous about sex.

"It's all good, River," he said. "I pity the male who ends up with that one."

Desiree made a face and shot Max the finger. "Get guarding, wolf."

He obligingly moved off, taking another huge sandwich with him, a package of sodas dangling from a finger.

"What exactly is he guarding against?"

"Jett and most of the males have gone out in teams to track down a group of rogues. If they can catch the leader they'll be ahead of the game."

Her appetite vanished and the food she'd eaten sat heavily in her stomach. Her old pack lived in relative harmony, and if there'd been an issue requiring a mobilization of force, it had been before her time. "I have no experience with that."

"We don't hold the safest territory, but most packs get challenged at some point, particularly younger ones like ours. Jericho's pack is established, and rogues are wary. But Jett will deal with it." Desiree almost sounded blasé about the situation. Almost.

"Are they going to be alright? The teams?" *Jett?*

Rising to clear their plates, Desiree gave her a hug first and River surprisingly clung to her voluptuous frame. "Hey. They'll be fine. For sure."

Staring into Desiree's face she realized for all her sister-in-law's lighthearted engagement, she was concerned and hiding it. "Desi. Tell me."

Putting the dishes in the sink, the other woman handed River a cloth to wipe down the counter. "Nothing's certain. But they have the upper hand, according to Tahl, so we shouldn't worry."

There was something in the way Desiree spoke the lieutenant's name… "Is Tahl *the* guy?"

"And you thought you weren't the perfect choice for Alpha's mate," Desi scoffed. "You're either a mind reader or—"

"It was the way you said his name."

"Oh. Well. It feels pretty good on my lips. He'd feel good on my lips."

They giggled and Desiree slung an arm over River's shoulder. River was laughing in part at the risqué comment to her shock, but also with relief. If Tahl had caught Desi's eye then that was one less male to worry about. She wondered how many single males were in Jett's immediate circle but didn't know how to broach the subject with Desi without an explanation. Would the Alpha's mate ask such things? Maybe it was okay to ask about pack configurations—

"We'll have coffee—tea for you—in the living

room, unless you want to have it in your room while you unpack?"

"I don't have anything I want you to see. I don't have a lot suitable to wear as Alpha's mate." She tasted the title again silently and figured she could accept it. "I'd be grateful if your help can extend to taking me shopping. Once the danger is over, that is."

"We aren't going to think about that right now. It's hard not to worry, but I'm sure it'll be over soon. And then I'll help you spend Jett's money!" Desiree handed her a cup.

"I have my own money," she protested, as she led the way to the living room.

"Don't challenge Jett on that, honey. He'll be insulted."

She knew how he responded to an insult, even an indirect, inadvertent one, so she nodded. "Okay. As long as you don't get me in trouble by overspending."

"Are you a frugal person, River?"

"I'm an accountant."

Desiree groaned, and then brightened. "Maybe you can help me set up a budget. Tahl is always giving me grief over spending in what he terms a frivolous manner." She frowned again. "He treats me like an inconvenient little sister sometimes."

"You want to change for him?" Her own fate made her ask the question.

"I think there's a certain amount of changing that has to take place. Not subjugation, if that's what you mean, by the look on your face. And of course being claimed has an impact on both parties. But learning to live within a budget is, overall, a good thing."

"Is there anything you would find … repulsive?"

Desiree's finely plucked brows climbed toward her hair line. "Do you mean sexually?"

Great. She just had to ask. River didn't talk about this stuff with anyone and had no idea how to do it with a relative stranger, no matter how much she was coming to like the young wolf. "Maybe."

"I want to try everything. But with Tahl. I'm not into casual."

TMI. "Everything?"

"Well, I have my fantasies and I hope he'll help me explore them."

"What about his fantasies?" River held her breath.

"I hope they'll mirror mine, but if not, I hope we'll figure it out. It's not like he'll—" Desiree's cell rang and she grabbed for it, stabbing at the screen. "Hello? What? Hang on."

Turning to River, she tucked the phone on the cushion. "Where's your phone? Jett's been calling you."

Crap. "Upstairs. I'll run and get it."

She flew up the steps, cursing the interruption because she was certain Desi was about to impart a revelation. *It's not like he'll expect me to say no? It's not like he'll want me to disappoint him?* She wanted to talk with another female about her biggest fear and maybe find a way to live with it. Except she knew she could never... She grabbed her phone from the dresser and stared at the screen. Four missed calls from her mate. *Wonderful impression, River.*

The device vibrated in her hand and she jumped, then answered.

"River. It'd be good if you carried your *mobile* phone with you."

"Sorry. I can hear it in my house no matter where I leave it. I didn't realize—"

"S'okay, sweetheart. You getting along with my sister? Did you eat?"

"Yes and yes."

He laughed. "Always a woman of few words unless you're having an outburst." He lowered his voice. "Are you okay?"

"Like in coping with my heat okay? Feeling okay or homesick? Feeling left in the dark about my mate out on some kind of dangerous mission okay?"

"River." A wealth of emotion poured through the phone. "You're worried. Sweetheart, it'll be fine. I'll be home soon."

She didn't deny her concern for him. She'd put it out there for anyone to hear. "I don't understand how I've become so attached in a day," she nearly whined, and wanted to pinch herself for her tone. Never mind feeling vulnerable.

"It goes both ways, sweetheart, if that helps. Which is why I called you. No one can fight destiny. This damn rogue incursion couldn't have happened at a worse time. I don't want you dealing with your heat on your own either."

So he wanted to be with her and not only to address her heat. A tendril of warmth totally unrelated to her hormonal urges unfurled in her chest. "I'll tell you, if, you know…" She didn't want to talk about sex. "And you be careful."

"I will. You listen to Max and spend time with Desi, okay? Get her to show you the safe room. You'll get a kick out of it."

Safe room? Lord. Maybe big ol' Max wasn't enough protection. She wanted to ask more questions but decided to obey him. *Trust him.* That felt better. "I'll ask her."

"Later, sweetheart."

"Later." She felt as though she should be saying something else but the screen darkened as he ended the call. Maybe she could come up with an endearment for him. Dear. Nope, too herbivore-ish. Baby? Too weird. Pumpkin? Ha. Lamb chop? She chuckled and it morphed into a sob.

"Hey, River. You done? Tahl said they're off to do male things." Desi's happy tone sounded forced to anyone's ear.

"I'm done," she called, and headed back down to the living room. "Jett said to show me the safe room."

"Really. Tahl too."

Max appeared in the doorway. "This way, ladies."

It appeared Max had his instructions as well, and a bunch of rocks rolled around in River's chest. What were Jett and the others dealing with and what about the rest of the pack still in the area? She asked Max.

"They're doing what has to be done, River. Jett will fill you in afterward. As for the rest of the pack, there's mostly females and pups, with a few like me remaining behind to pull up the drawbridge in case."

"In case?"

"Cornered prey can be unpredictable, particularly *thinking* cornered prey. So everybody's heading into safe rooms or traveling."

Wordless, she accompanied Desiree and Max down a short set of stairs beside the kitchen. A door with a keypad loomed at the bottom and Max punched in a code, and then pulled the metal panel open. For all of its obvious weight, it swung open noiselessly and they moved inside. It closed behind them with a quiet thud and she looked around.

"Bathroom that way." Max pointed. "Foodstuffs and water stored there. Blankets in that cupboard."

There was a television and some seating, a DVD player and a shelf of movies. River felt for her phone and determined she had service. A bank of monitors flickered on one wall and she recognized various screenshots of inside the house. Jett's bedroom was on the top upper left and she blinked.

"Is there any other place in the house that displays the security camera feed?" she asked Max. *Were you watching your Alpha and me earlier?*

"No. Only in the safe room. Jett is practical but likes his privacy."

"Right." She looked away casually.

"Chic flic!" Desiree plucked a movie and flicked open the package. She slid it into the player and grabbed the remote. "Sit with me, River, and we'll immerse ourselves while Max suffers."

He grunted and pulled out his phone. "I'll play a game. Over here."

"So we just wait?" River asked.

"Uh huh." Desiree poked at buttons.

"Do you do this often?" She was safe and sound in some basement bunker while her mate was … not.

"Nope. My first time." River could hear the worry bubbling in Desi's voice despite her focus on the remote.

Tugging the device from the other woman's hand, she started the movie. "We should have made popcorn."

Desi snuggled beside her and they watched some incredibly talented dancers from decades ago liven up a summer camp while the hero dealt with maligning rumors. If River stared hard enough, she could pretend the hours would fly by like that girl leaping from the stage into the gorgeous hero's arms.

Chapter Six

"Fuck." Jett swiped a hand over his face, wincing at the split in his right eyebrow. Blood coated his fingers and he wiped most of it off on his shirt. The cut—and one bitch of a headache—was the only damage he'd sustained and he considered himself lucky. Tahl had a broken arm and severe bruising along his ribs from a stray bullet, and they'd lost five males with another, so injured it was a toss-up as to whether he'd make it or not. They'd gotten him to their medic but only time would tell.

Jett knew the price of battle, but losing members of his pack took pieces of his soul. He made a major effort to focus on the next step and considered the remaining members of the teams. Most suffered some minor cuts and bruises, and the rogues were down by at least three-quarters of their number, thanks to the intel. Taking the enemy by surprise had proven to be an incredible advantage, except the alpha rogue had escaped. Rees and Davis were on his trail, having blooded him, and Jett hoped they were successful because a male like that would simply rebuild. And revenge would drive him.

"Too bad we don't heal lightning quick like the books say," Tahl grunted. "My fucking arm is killing me."

"Compound fractures do that." Jett checked the splint again to make sure the break was aligned. He didn't want to have to break his lieutenant's arm a second time because shifters did, in fact, heal quickly, just not miraculously.

"Your head okay? That bat caught you a good one."

"The asshole wielding the bat caught me," he retorted. "He came out of nowhere. Like a crazy man. I'm good, though. If I hadn't been in wolf form, maybe not." He'd torn the attacker's throat out and wished there had been another choice.

"I expect he was on some kind of synth medication. We found a lab in the basement. Guess it's another way the rogue alpha keeps his followers tight."

Kris wobbled into view, having lost some blood after suffering a bite to the thigh. The rogues had fought, both shifted, and in human form. The latter had used human weapons, though the firepower had been limited. Jett figured he should be grateful for small mercies.

"Any word on the Regent?" He could have bitten his tongue. He shouldn't give that asshole any kind of title or recognition. "The leader?"

"He's circling. Getting closer to our territory, actually."

"Then order the teams home. If he joins up with the others we put on the road, I don't want our people in their path without the best defense." Even if they were in safe rooms and the like. He helped Tahl to his feet.

"The females are ready for transport, Jett." Kris's lip curled with rage. They were all disgusted at the way the rogues had treated the female wolves, but Kris was having a really hard time managing his anger. "A couple of them, the ones in the best shape, will kind of direct the rest."

"Set them up where we discussed, Kris. We can't risk any having fallen prey to Stockholm."

"The things you have to foresee, Jett." Kris gave him a respectful nod and headed out.

Tahl said, "You can't believe any female would be attached to a male who would treat her the way those women have been treated?"

"If any of them were in heat, who knows? Males have the control in that instance, Tahl. And females surrender." River's surrender, overwhelmed by her wolf's need, despite her strong will to the contrary flashed before his eyes, and he frowned. They really needed to talk so he could uncover the root of her antipathy, though their phone conversation had lifted his spirits. He was more than physically connected to his little mate—and she to him if he'd read her concern correctly. It was the way of fated mates.

"I suppose so. And it's fucking wrong to manipulate nature that way. All the more reason to ensure we don't have rogue wolves." Tahl made his way toward the vehicle, his injured ribs making his movements stiff. When he eased into the passenger seat, he turned to face Jett. "Now might not be the best time, Jett. Or maybe it is, seeing as you're mated now."

Jett braced himself for what he knew was coming. He prided himself on paying attention and knowing what was going on in his pack. It didn't mean he didn't have a moment's pause when he thought of his sister being in River's position. Not that he didn't support destiny, but Desiree was still a little girl in his head.

"She's really interested, Tahl. And I couldn't pick a better man for Desiree. If you want my permission to connect, you have it."

His lieutenant tensed. "Fuck. Son of a…" His green eyes showed wolf and Jett's animal coiled in response. Tahl took a deep breath and winced. "I am so fucked. With you *and* her. Did I give out some kind of message?"

"I don't follow."

"You said Desi's interested. Jett, I don't reciprocate."

"Holy hell." He searched his recent memory of

the interaction between Tahl and Desiree and concluded the sexual interest was one sided, except all the single males got a little more bulked up when she flirted. It was a natural response. "No, you haven't been giving mixed messages. But it's gonna be a mess. Fuck me. Maybe I can find some business to follow up on elsewhere. Far away."

With a pained laugh, Tahl replied, "Nothing like an upset she-wolf to make us all head for the hills. But seriously, I feel bad. I tried hard not to give her any encouragement."

"I know how Desiree is, my friend. Once she gets an idea in her head there's no changing that single-minded focus. I didn't notice your response—or lack thereof—because I don't want to think about her…"

"Getting mated?" His lieutenant chose the kinder description of what Jett and River had enjoyed.

"Right. I'll break it to her sooner than later."

"I probably should do it. She'll be humiliated enough, don't you think? I mean she's a great kid, but that's how I see her."

"Maybe hearing it from you will make it clear. She might think I'm interfering and come to you anyhow. But if you didn't want to talk to me about Desi, then what?"

Tahl visibly collected his thoughts. "I want your leave to attend another pack. As soon as the current crisis is resolved."

"Any particular pack?"

"Ashton Leaf's. The Dawnfall Pack. There's a female there who'll be coming up to her first heat and I want to be first in the running. If you and Ashton can see your way clear."

"Do I know her?"

"She was with Ashton and his entourage a couple

of years ago when they passed through. You probably recall her. The redhead?"

Jett vaguely remembered a little princess of a she-wolf flitting around and thought it was her who had stirred some trouble with her peers among his pack. Something about comparing assets. Not that Ashton and his people had stayed that long, and he'd been caught up in hammering out an alliance with the other alpha. "I remember."

"Well, I saw her and … well, I haven't forgotten, you know?"

He didn't know, being that River was the first female to have an impact on him—in that way. "And if she's suitable? How long will you be gone?"

Discomfort etched Tahl's face and it wasn't all from his injuries. "Ashton would expect that I stay. It's his granddaughter. Peyton. And I want to court her, so…"

Damn it. He really didn't want to lose his lieutenant. He could forbid Tahl, but didn't have a good reason, and while the other man would accept his edict, resentment would only fester. "I can't say as I want her to be suitable."

A bark of laughter made Tahl most definitely wince and he used his good hand to compress his ribs. "I figured. But you'll give permission?"

"Right after you break the news to Desiree."

"I wasn't going to take off without telling her, Jett. Especially now I understand she's sincere about her focus on me."

He knew the other man was better than that, but he was pissed at him too. How was he going to replace him?

"Kris could step up," Tahl suggested, reading Jett's mind the way he often did.

"Not Kris."

"You might not like him personally, but he's the best one for the position."

"We'll see." Not that he had a lot of time to decide.

He started the vehicle and began the drive back to his territory, cell phone at the ready to keep in touch with the forward teams. "You'll let me know if congratulations are in order, Tahl."

"I will. And we'll make a point of connecting afterward. Maybe our mates will become friends." Jett doubted it, despite only a vague impression of Peyton. River wasn't a flirt and she didn't aspire to material things.

None of the teams called with news of the rogue alpha. Rees and Davis concluded someone had picked him up because the trail had gone cold. It wasn't optimum although Rees suggested the male had been driven out of familiar territory and would have to set up a camp elsewhere, further away. His ragtag pack decimated, the likelihood of him gathering a large enough number to pose a threat to any lawful pack was far in the future.

"They aren't really rogues," Tahl observed.

Startled, Jett threw his lieutenant a glance. "How do you figure?"

"They have—had—a pack and followed an alpha. Kind of like the one percenters of a motorcycle gang. I mean, most packs follow pack law with some minor variations, but essentially avoid a lot of the shit we got mired in before progress paved the way. The better way."

"That so-called Alpha demanded loyalty at the threat of death. Not to mention he encouraged violence against others and encouraged and supplied drugs to cement those ties. And let's not forget the harem."

"Beyond the pale," Tahl agreed. "Twisted and sick, but still a pack. What's to say he won't rebuild better and stronger and become a force we have to negotiate with?"

"That's not going to happen. Not on my watch. And I'll shout out to the rest of the Alphas we're connected with already and have them do the same to others. We'll conference if need be, but I can't see any pack I know standing for such a travesty. And this is why I need you as my lieutenant, Tahl." He thumped the dash in frustration.

"You'd have come to it. I expect it's the lure of your little mate that's derailed your thinking a tad."

"I haven't been on my game in quite the same way," he admitted.

"No, that's not right. You are, if anything, heightened, so far as your intuition goes. Probably because your protective instincts are at an all-time high. You saved my ass back there, Jett. You know it."

"We have one another's backs."

"Right. Well, you have my thanks anyhow. And as for my recent epiphany, it's what you pay me for."

He cruised into Tahl's driveway and pulled as close to the house as possible. "I'll expect you tomorrow after lunch. I'll make sure Desiree is there. Unless you want to go to Mom's house. She should be back—"

"Uh, no. Your mother will skin me alive."

"She'll come to the same conclusion as me, though maybe it's best she's not there when you break the news."

Climbing slowly out of the vehicle, the other male grimaced. "I'm sick about it, Jett, but it's gotta be done. And the sooner the better. I won't head out for Ashton's pack though until I'm sure things are settled here."

"Deal." Jett made sure Tahl got inside before pulling a three point turn and heading home. He and River needed some time alone. His wolf hoped that meant time spent in a most pleasurable manner, but he knew they should cover some other areas first before he covered her.

His house came into view and he automatically scanned for anything out of the ordinary. It was no secret—to wolves anyway—where he lived, and while Max hadn't communicated with him, since the order to hit the safe room, other than to say things were copacetic, Jett was always prepared for the unexpected. Except for River.

He smiled happily, even thinking about her, despite the fact the two of them would have to make trips to the families of the wolves who'd lost their lives. His mate would be dropped head first into her role and under unpleasant circumstances. Yet he had no doubt she'd be up to the task.

The thought of Tahl courting the little redhead crossed his mind. Would it have been better to have courted River? With an inner snort, he discarded the idea. No way would he have gotten her to cooperate, considering how resistant and flighty she behaved. The blitzkrieg had been the best choice, even if he had reacted on instinct alone.

Disarming the system, he kicked off his boots and strode to the small bathroom on the main floor. He wanted to clean up before he saw River. Desiree would be looking for information about Tahl, and he wished he'd given that a little more thought.

He dunked his face into a sink full of cool water and then scrubbed his hands, the residual moisture leaking into his collar. Using a hand towel, he dried off, compressing one eye at the blood stains he left behind before tossing it under the sink.

"Jett?" He'd scented and heard her long before she spoke but had a little tussle with his wolf so as not to jump her.

She stood hesitantly in the doorway and for a second he wondered how the rest of the pack would view her because she presented as so unprepossessing. There was no outward sign of her strong will or of the young girl who'd raised up a much younger sister. A sister who clearly adored River. Jericho knew her worth, but the male was privy to all the members of his pack. Their history, their education, and their current employment. He imagined it had pinched his sire to lose someone with such financial acumen, so Jericho had thought long and hard before suggesting her.

He liked her hints of sarcasm and feistiness— when she wasn't challenging what was tried and true pack law—and sensed the nurturing heart behind the fear and anxiety. Something he was going to deal with in the very near future.

But as all of that passed through his head, he was on the move to pull her close. She melted into him. Part of it was the mating heat but not all. His little mate had indeed been worried about him and craving his presence. He doubted it was only because she saw him as being her protector in a strange place—or so he hoped.

"Hey, sweetheart." He noted the scent of her, apple shampoo and River. If pressed to describe it, he'd have to say, rich, warm and earthy with a touch of cinnamon. Her small body fit against him like a missing puzzle piece and his wolf purred throatily while his cock filled. Fresh arousal perfumed the air and he ruthlessly tamped down his response.

"Is it all over?" she asked, her voice muffled by his shirt.

"For now. We scattered them. At a cost, but it had to be done."

She leaned back and peered up at him. "What kind of cost?"

"Several of our males are down. Five to be exact, and possibly another."

Dark brown eyes filled with moisture and a solitary tear escaped. He brushed it away with his thumb and let himself feel the loss of his pack members keenly. River winced in concert and pressed closer, in tune despite the short term of their connection. "I'm so sorry."

"We'll have to go tomorrow and see their families."

"All right."

Setting her a little distance away, he said, "The rogues held seventeen females."

She shivered. "Are they... What shape are they in?"

"Not great. Physically we can expect them to heal. Emotionally... Well, things like that take time." *Forever.* "I'm going to ask you to work out a plan for them, as my mate."

"I don't know, Jett. I—"

"I'll help you," Desiree spoke quietly, but he heard the judgment in her voice. And so did River by the way she tugged away and turned to face his sister.

"I'll do my best, Desiree. But it ... that kind of thing ... I don't want to make it worse."

"Assure them they're safe and we'll get them home, or let them stay in our pack as valued members," he suggested. "That's a start."

"Right." She nodded but kept her gaze on his sister. Desiree stared back before looking at him.

"Who were killed?"

He shared the names, including the male who was

under medical care, and Desi looked relieved, and then ashamed. She cast another glance at River before asking, "Do you want me to come with you in the morning?"

"No. River and I will handle it. You and Mom can help her figure out the details for family support later. River's an accountant so she'll be an asset in that regard too. I do want you here tomorrow afternoon."

"Oh?"

"After lunch."

Desi's eyebrows drew together, but she didn't question him further. "River and I are getting to know one another, Jett." Her tone suggested she wasn't necessarily enamored with his mate, and he gave her a warning look.

River's shoulders slumped, and she visibly retreated from Desiree. His sister gave a casual wave and turned on her heel to saunter away. Jett called for Max to escort his sister to her car, before focusing again on his mate.

"River? What happened between you and Desi?" If there was an issue between her and his family, it was going to draw some lines in the sand.

"She's disappointed in me. You saw it." She turned to face him, pretty face set in a rueful frown.

"I don't understand your reticence either," he admitted. "But as your mate, we're going to talk about it and I'm not going to flounce out the door like a little princess." He wished he'd said something to Desiree to correct that attitude, but he had to find out what was operating with his mate first.

"I'm sorry for those females." Her lips compressed and she blinked furiously but couldn't hold the tears back.

"Sweetheart." He wrapped her up, escorting her out of the bathroom.

Through her sobs, she stuttered, "I … I am sorry. You don't know how sorry. It's awful."

"And they need input and support. Who better than the Alpha's mate?"

"I couldn't help my mother." If bitterness was a weapon, she'd have battered him with it.

"Your mother was abused?"

"You can say it, Jett. Rape. Raped. Just because she wasn't taken by rogues and used, it doesn't change the facts."

"But your father—"

"Perpetrated it!" With a strength he would have doubted she possessed, she tore free and rushed ahead into the kitchen, him hard on her heels.

He headed her off and cornered her against the end cabinet. "Breathe," he commanded, as he ran his hands up and down her arms.

She took a few shuddering breaths but wouldn't look at him. He leaned in and rested his forehead against hers. When her breathing mirrored his, he slipped an arm around her shoulders and guided her to a stool at the counter. She sat and folded her hands on the edge, weaving her slender fingers together. He went and rifled through the pantry, finding a box of tea bags he knew his sister enjoyed. With honey.

River sat silently while he microwaved a cup of water and dipped a bag in, letting it steep until it was a golden color. He added a dollop of sweetness and stirred the mixture after discarding the bag. The process gave him time to collect his thoughts and suppress the urge to head straight back to Jericho's territory to kill her father and confront his sire on the rot within his pack.

"Here you go."

Working her fingers loose, she set both hands around the cup as if seeking comfort. She lifted it carefully and took a sip, then another. "Thank you."

Max hovered in the doorway, a worried frown on his face. He mouthed, "She okay?"

Jett put a hand up, out of River's field of vision, and the big male eased out of sight. A short while later, a beep sounded and the front door closed. Ever careful, Max had locked them in and armed the system. He knew he could trust the man to keep quiet about whatever he overheard, and from the look Max gave him, he was concerned for River. He intuited the man liked her as well. It was too bad about Desi.

"Talk to me, sweetheart. Let me in."

"What's there to say? Wolves share. Mated wolves share their females. It's accepted and touted as normal. Except there are females who don't want to be shared."

"Right." He obviously wasn't getting it. He tried to reframe it. "Wolves have sex in a variety of configurations, right up to a mating claim. We aren't a judgmental species, River, for sure. But it's consensual, because if it isn't, the perpetrators are dealt with severely."

She shook her head. "I know that." She blushed, and he nearly had to sit on his hands not to run a finger down one soft cheek and distract her, now she was opening up. "I don't care what others *choose* to do once they come of age to uh, consort with others."

Consort? He supposed it was as good a word as any, though his consorting had been more like fucking his way through a swath of interested females. Sometimes he and Tahl double teamed a willing bedmate, and while it was an experience, it wasn't something he required. "I don't follow, River. Are you saying your dad raped your mother and was still allowed to claim her?"

"No. Lord, I don't want to talk about this. I don't want to think about it—it makes me remember."

"It's getting between us," he said patiently. "And impacting your role as my mate. You obviously remember, so talking it out might help. Desiree was out of line because she made a snap judgment. She's under some ... stress, but we need to straighten things out between you and her."

"She's your family. I know."

"You're my family too, and you come first."

Wide-eyed, she compressed her lips before saying, "I don't want to come between you and your mother and sisters. I don't."

"Then enlighten me. It's killing me River, that you won't open up and let me help you. Let me in, sweetheart."

She took a huge breath. The cup of tea shook between her hands and he laid a hand on her arm, taking it as a good sign that she didn't rebuff him. Another deep breath lifted her breasts and he resolutely didn't stare. "My father invited single males over on a regular basis. To be with my mother. Cass and I were always in bed, but I heard them. I think she slept through it. I hope she did."

"And your mother didn't wish it?" Single males like Kris would happily share River, but only if necessary and she consented. And thus far it didn't appear necessary. It was a tried and true method to assuage an out-of-control heat, rather than involving their doctors and utilizing medication with severe side effects. Not that he'd choose Kris for her.

"She begged and pleaded with my father and ... whoever came over. I never met them though I recognized some voices."

"Did you hear her refuse? Call for help? Did you

see injuries, River?"

"Just the noises. Her crying out, but I guess I didn't hear any specific words. And she looked okay in the morning, though tired. She seemed tired all the time."

"How did she die?"

"A blood disease. Rare for lupines and incurable. I looked it up when I got older because I wondered if it was genetic. It's not." She sounded much calmer and paused to take a sip of tea. "I couldn't understand why she didn't do something, like complain to our Alpha. Or even leave. Except then I realized my dad had all the power, and she was bound by her heat."

He chose his words carefully because a lot rested on how she received the information. He resisted the urge to rub his chest where a cold ache had set in. If he wasn't enough for River, no matter if she came to understand that what took place in some instances was necessary, he doubted she would get past her entrenched beliefs. At least not right away, and he couldn't imagine the impact it would have on their connection, not to mention if her heat spiraled out of control.

"Are you aware if a female's heat can't be totally assuaged by their mates, inviting other males to, uh, assist, is common? Necessary. Far better than hormone-suppressing drugs that can cause mood disorders, infertility, or miscarriage."

"What?" There was enough incredulity packed into one short word that he flinched in the face of it.

"Truth, River."

She stared in shock, unblinking, and every vestige of color drained from her face. A harsh swallow wracked her slender throat and she choked on it. "So it wasn't to satisfy my father's kink?" A small hand pressed against her lips as if to contain any further words. A tiny moan escaped before she spoke again. "But she had to put up with it, even if she didn't want it? To conceive the sons *he* wanted?"

"I can't begin to guess, but she might have wanted them—the sons—too."

"Right. Male children." Antipathy and scorn dripped from the words, and Jett momentarily wished he was the opposite gender. In his mind, despite the specifics of gender roles, males and females were as important as the other. But River had grown up with terrible childhood memories and her grasp of mating was twisted because of it. How was it that she lacked that key component?

"We're not so bad," he tried.

There was no softness in her face when she looked at him. "What if you can't sate my heat? Because it's coming back worse than before. I can feel it. I can't let you bring someone else in. I won't."

"You're over-reacting," he soothed. "We can't know how things will go." His belly clenched to the point of pain when he even considering sharing her and his wolf howled so loudly his ears popped.

Her elbow caught the mug and sent it crashing to the floor as River threw herself off the stool and raced away. Leaving the mess, he ran after her. She flew up the stairs and only a final burst of speed caught the bedroom door before she slammed it shut.

"Running won't address the issue."

"I guess not," she bit out. "I can't run far enough, thanks to you."

He reached for control, but his wolf had responded to the chase. Despite the emotional blows, his mate's heat was escalating. "Show some respect, River."

New color leached from her face. "I'm sorry. You had an awful two days and I'm adding to it. But it was too much to take in. I can't think it through. I'm scared."

Wolf roiling right at the surface, he stared her down. "Come here. Do not make me come to you. After you. My wolf isn't discriminating between your heat and your angst."

She pattered over and looked up at him. With a gentle finger she touched his healing cut and it nearly undid him. But he wove his fingers through her wealth of hair, knowing not to let her distract him. She liked the dominant touch whether she'd admit it or not, or at least her wolf did, to judge by the immediate increase in her arousal. When she sagged a little, he tightened his grip and pulled, watching her eyes dilate. "You're not to retreat into your head. Do you understand? You stay with me and go all in. We're going to get through this. Together. Just you and me."

Her pink, pointed tongue whipped over her biteable bottom lip and he speculated how it would feel on the head of his cock. The touch of her fingers over the ridge of his erection managed to redirect his thoughts. He shoved his hips into her hands and nearly came in his jeans when she stroked him while fumbling for the zipper. She hopefully wouldn't catch something important in the jagged teeth.

Delving behind the waistband, she closed a hand around him and he groaned. "Careful, sweetheart. I've done without since yesterday."

Locking her gaze on his, she stroked from root to head, feathering a nail over the sensitive corona before dipping lower to cradle his balls and squeeze them gently. He wouldn't let himself wonder where she'd learned that, but instead gave over to the sensation until he had to stop her. "I want to be inside of you."

He swore his cock shivered at the loss of her touch—for damn sure it wept—and he yanked at her clothes, his jeans slipping to fall around his ankles.

Tugging her bra down to plump those sweet mounds into perfect position for his mouth, he took advantage, alternately suckling the beaded nubs hard and fast. River whimpered and arched against him, her own jeans loosened and working over her hips.

Somehow, he got her turned and bent over the side of the bed, the stricture of clothing impeding his movements, but he couldn't spare another second. River was hobbled at the knees, and he worked a hand between her thighs to test her readiness. Drenched. He drove between her thighs and glided into her folds to find her opening. Impossibly tight in this position, she still opened to him and he inched inside. "Fuck, you feel so good. Made for my cock."

Relishing the snug, velvet grip of her, he nuzzled up her spine. Gooseflesh bloomed in his wake until he reached the juncture of her graceful neck and slender shoulder. He placed his mouth over his claiming mark and sucked as his hips bucked and retreated against the curve of her ass. Wet, slapping sounds proclaimed their joining and he tried to make it last. River came hard around him, squeezing with a long, liquid draw. His cum burst forth and he bit down at the intensity of it. This little woman fucking well did it for him and he'd frazzle the skin off his cock and pump himself dry and aching before another male touched her.

Furiously jealous, his wolf howling in wild agreement, he pulled her in tight, his teeth releasing her tender flesh. "No more running. No more avoidance. You're mine, River. Accept it and lose those fears."

Chapter Seven

Pinned beneath her mate's bulk, his cock still pulsing inside of her and his renewed bite tingling, River tried to open her mind and take his words to heart. It was difficult to process through the residual sensations of another body-clenching orgasm, but she registered the depth of feeling in his proclamation. She badly wanted to believe him, believe he could circumvent nature and that she wouldn't be one of those females who had needs too great for her mate to meet—without help.

There was no way the fault would lie with a potent male like Jett. Her mother's disease wasn't genetic but River might have inherited that insatiable heat issue. Cass too. She needed to call her sister—and tell her what? She couldn't even talk to her mate without falling apart. "I have to talk to Cass. She might inherit the heat problem. Too."

"Fuck me." Jett pulled out of her and she winced. She was soaked and no doubt her clothes were ruined again. Her bra was stretched around her waist and her nice top seemed to be in pieces.

He knelt beside her and peeled her out of her remaining clothing, kicking free of his jeans. That monster cock crouched along his thigh and she tore her gaze away in case it woke up again. She felt sated for now but damn tender. When he mopped her up with a wad of tissues, she wanted to put a pillow over her face. The intimacies were something she might never get used to.

"Listen to me." His tone brooked no disobedience.

She looked him in the face and paid attention.

"Do you even *know* if it's hereditary?" he asked.

"Uh, no. But I hadn't even heard of it until now."

"Exactly. River, you have a brain. You're smart when you aren't reacting from some place in your gut that stores all the scary things. Just so you're aware, it's not actually that common, at least not in our pack."

"That you know of."

He hesitated, as though choosing his words carefully. "I do know, River. I'm the Alpha, remember?

She frowned. "I'd have thought you'd hold the female responsible."

Jett slumped back and threw his forearm over his eyes, muttering about needing strength. She cautiously felt her neck, where the bite throbbed a little, and he somehow knew. "Did I hurt you?"

"No. If anything, it made me … come harder," she admitted.

"That's something then."

He was teasing her again. She was figuring him out—and she kinda liked it. "Something." *Take that.*

"Wench." He wrapped her up and rolled her partially under him, staring into her eyes. "Now, listen. You have this unbalanced take on male and female roles in regard to mates. Yes, the male becomes more dominant, and obedience by the female—submission and surrender—is a huge turn on for us. At least in the bedroom. Females embrace our protection and the nurturing because historically we were all that stood between them, the pups and the big, bad world.

"But blame isn't levied about the mating heat. You don't cast blame on nature. We do whatever is necessary to assuage that need, and if we fall short, we fix it. Is it a slam to the ego? It could be if the male is arrogant enough to think he can circumvent a natural issue, something beyond control, but generally, a male doesn't think that way. He'll do anything for his mate.

Can't you see that? The mating heat has ensured our survival for centuries, River, and if we let ego and blame get in the way, we're dooming our species."

"I feel like I grew up under a rock." Though she still couldn't even entertain the idea of another male touching her.

"I'll bet there's an explanation for that. What happened after your mom died?"

"My dad forgot about us. For a long time. Oh, he took care of us financially, but it was like he couldn't even stand to see us. It was really hard on Cass."

"Not you?"

"No. I already had a bad opinion of him and his rejection was okay."

"Really?"

A sudden rush of tears burned her eyes. "No. I guess not. If I let myself really consider it I felt totally abandoned. But I had Cass to worry about, so I coped."

"You were fucking well ten years old. A baby in shifter years. You lost your mom and you miss her no matter how confused you were about some things you overheard. Christ sake, River. Give yourself some credit."

"It's done, Jett." It hurt too much to do more than hear his words. She would do some thinking over the next while—cautiously.

"But you can give it some thought and see what you lost and maybe we can replace some of that."

He was a freaking mind reader. Tears escaped and she snuffled into her hand. Jett passed her some tissues and rubbed her back. Her wolf relaxed into his touch and ... so did she. "I'll try."

"I'll help. Because I'm not letting you slip back."

As she settled, he posed another question. "So you learned about mating and wolf intimacy from your mom as much as she could share at that age?"

"Right. Generalities only, but I knew what I heard those nights. Then I heard things at school. Humans are quite different than wolves and the freedom their females experienced drew me. I guess I was so busy avoiding wolf sexual culture that I confused myself."

"I'd say so," he said drily. "And from here on in, you're going to ask *me*. And what I don't know—from the female side of things—I'll have an older female fill you in."

"Maybe your Mom? If Desiree hasn't already made her hate me."

"Leave Desi to me. She'll have her own issues to deal with tomorrow."

"Why?"

He sighed and she again regretted how she hadn't acted like an adult given the huge burden he carried. They could have talked it out before he'd... Ah, and now she was accepting they'd have sex before or after or whenever. She still felt a twinge of resentment he had interrupted her foray into independence, but it was being consumed by other, more interesting feelings. Maybe more palatable ones. And then there was the issue of being considered a rogue...

"Desi has her heart set on Tahl." Jett pulled her into the present.

"I know," she agreed. "She told me."

"So you did connect."

"We did until I freaked out about helping those females. She must think I'm a terrible person and not fit to be your mate."

"My sister is spoiled and a bit self-absorbed, and doesn't always consider all the implications before she reacts."

Like me. She was glad he didn't make the

comparison and focused on his next statement.

"But she has a good heart and will come around. Maybe you could share a bit with her, because despite her other failings, she absolutely can keep her mouth shut."

"We nearly touched on my ... issues today, but life intervened. So why is she going to be upset?"

"Tahl doesn't want her."

"Oh, no." She felt Desiree's anticipated pain. "Oh, dear."

"He's heading to another pack and if the female is amenable to his claim he'll remain there."

"Another female? Poor Desi."

"He hasn't led her on, River. Not at all. It's all one-sided."

"I don't know if that's better or worse. And he's not coming back? I thought he was your lieutenant? Are you going to tell her?"

"No. Tahl is. He believes it's the right thing to do. And as for losing him, think of what it would mean if I denied him leave."

She couldn't imagine how that was going to play out tomorrow and wished she didn't have to be around to see it. But she was the alpha's mate and needed to start thinking that way. "I'll see if she'll help me with a plan for those seventeen women. It might ease her a little. Distract her."

Jett nodded, but she felt his worry. Desiree was going to be broken hearted—and humiliated. The younger female had over a year to her mating heat, however, and hopefully, by then, someone worthy would catch her eye to replace Tahl. He'd claim her and it would all be good. Like with her and Jett.

Totally shocked, she shoved up to a sitting position and dragged her tangled hair out of her face. Jett stared back at her.

"What?"

"I … I had this thought. That someone good for Desi would claim her and it would all work out. Like us."

His craggy features softened and he reached to place his hand over her heart. The warmth of his callused palm sank in deep. "It will work out, little River. Have faith."

"I do." She sank back down and cuddled close. Intellectually she knew it was his claim that was breaking down barriers between them—nature at work—but Jett had made a huge effort to facilitate the process. And if it was true and they were fated mates, it seemed more than she deserved. He might even come to love her, something she hoped was true, because she suspected it wouldn't be difficult to lose her heart to this many-layered man.

"My mother may not be the best choice to answer your questions, sweetheart."

"Why's that?" she asked drowsily, not really caring.

"Because she's human."

All weariness gone, she again heaved up and stared.

"Conversation stopper, eh?" He watched her warily before his gaze dropped lower. If it wasn't for the bombshell he'd just dropped, she might have smiled at the way he dragged his gaze back to communicate with her. Very reluctantly. She might be a pretty ordinary shifter, but Jett found her to his liking.

The implication of his mother's humanness hit hard. "Maybe you could have told me tomorrow. Or another time in the far future. My head is going to explode."

"You'll meet her tomorrow in all likelihood and

you'll see it. I didn't want to withhold."

"Right. Okay. So, Jericho mated a human." Her oh-so-traditional former Alpha.

"Not exactly mated. He had sex with her and she conceived. Not unheard of, but pretty damn rare. And here I am. And my birth changed something in her makeup because she connected with another wolf—my sisters' father, afterward. That was closer to a true mate bond." His face tightened. "It was fucking hard that he died while defending my territory."

There was so much to take in, but she focused on Jett. "Desiree is proud of him for doing his job, if that's any consolation."

"Some. My mother feels the same, but it weighs heavily on me."

Her heart pounded in her chest at the way he was opening up to her, and she tried to build a little distance so she wouldn't get all emotional and be unable to say the right thing. She wondered what his lineage was, given his parents. "So that makes you..."

"Part wolf. More human. And something else."

"Something else?" she whispered. So much for distance.

"My mother must have Fae blood, though there's no overt evidence of it and it's not like we have anyone to ask. The Fae have been gone from this realm for over a century. But whatever she passed on to me, I was destined for alpha status from day one. I walked, talked, and developed quicker than any of my peers, in addition to other things."

"How old are you?" There was so much she didn't know about him.

"Thirty-two."

"What? No!" She'd pegged him to be in his late forties, although it was difficult to know a wolf's age because they didn't seem to get older after forty or so. "You're so ... mature."

He shrugged. "Partly my upbringing, partly my genes. I finished college—I earned a degree in politics and what might be loosely called war mongering from a military institution—when I was seventeen. They thought I was twenty when I enrolled and doing five years in three isn't unheard of. Life experience is a great teacher too."

"I have to sleep on this, Jett. I can't seem to keep my eyes open." It was true. Her brain was shutting down as though someone was throwing light switches, one by one.

"We'll talk tomorrow," he promised, tucking her in beside him and dropping a kiss on her cheek. His cock throbbed against her hip, at full mast, and she felt a stirring of response. She made a mental note to ask him why he hadn't chosen a mate before now, and then mental exhaustion pulled her under.

****

Waking, she registered the empty space beside her. Considering how she'd never actually shared a bed with anyone before, she thought she could get used to it. But only if it was Jett sleeping there. *Not just sleeping.*

Arousal pricked the length of her spine and she chewed her bottom lip. Damn wolf. There were a few days to go before her hormones settled, but she was certain the need had leveled off to some extent—after yesterday's sex. Before it had simmered in the background where she'd been viscerally and painfully aware of it despite all efforts to distract herself. Now it was more like a sweet, anticipatory thrum. Perhaps it had been the education bestowed on her by her mate, settling her brain.

She'd processed a considerable amount

overnight. At some point, in the not so distant future, she needed to talk with her father. Not that she was going to open up that untouchable subject with him—no kids wanted to talk about sex with their parents. But maybe she could view him differently and perhaps they could connect in a healthier fashion. She wasn't going to give a moment's thought to being in the same position as her mother.

Today promised to be one full of heartache of all sorts, and she resolved to put her own issues aside and stand with Jett. Desiree was another consideration, and she hoped she and her sister-in-law might repair the blow to their burgeoning friendship. And then there was Jett's mom... Well, she'd form her own opinions when she met the woman.

Slipping from the bed, she located her robe and pulled it on, the plush fabric easing the chill of the room. Wolves ran hot and their homes were usually kept at a temperature below that of what humans found comfortable, but the bedroom was chilly by anyone's standards. Smoothing back her hair, she wandered to the head of the stairs and confirmed the faint noises she'd heard were confined to the kitchen.

Jett stood at the stove, poking at the bacon frying in the big skillet. Coffee gurgled into the pot on the counter beside him, the comforting sound warring with the aggressive sizzle of the meat, and a carton of eggs sat at his elbow.

"You cook too?"

He set the fork down and came to her, a pair of low slung shorts clinging to his hips. Every muscle and ridge on his torso stood out starkly and the 'V' framing his chiseled abdomen made her breath shorten.

Cradling her face between his big palms, he kissed her nose. She breathed in the smells of bacon and a freshly showered Jett, not that the soap masked his heady underlying scent.

"I'm a wolf of many talents, though breakfast is pretty much the ceiling as far as food goes. Morning, sweetheart." He drifted his fingers over her robe. "Lambs? Really?"

White sheep on a pink background had amused her, so she bought the cozy garment. "You're seeing my dark side."

With a chuckle, he pinched the fabric and drew her to the island. "Sit. I'll pour you a coffee and then scramble the eggs if that suits you? Toast is in the oven, staying warm. I thought you'd sleep forever."

"I need a lot of sleep. Always have. And scrambled is fine."

"Good to know. And you needed the rest."

She blushed, and he laughed again, stirring the eggs. "You've had a few nerve-wracking days, River. Although I did work you hard last night."

Would she ever get used to his plain speaking? Not to mention how his reference immediately set off her imagination. Her wolf was already awake and pacing, merely from seeing him. She reminded herself of what this morning held and held out her cup for more coffee, shoving everything else to the back of her mind.

"What time are we going to see the families, Jett?"

"Mid-morning. The last wolf, Johann, pulled through."

"A blessing," she said, and he gave her a small smile that didn't hide the pain he carried over the loss of the others.

They ate quickly, and he sent her up to shower and dress while he cleaned up. Her father hadn't lifted a finger in the house since her mother died, and River thought Jett's obvious domestication was something she could get used to. When she emerged from the bathroom, he was already dressed.

He approved of her simple suit, one she'd purchased to wear for her new job. "You look extremely professional. Like a serious librarian."

"Maybe I should wear my reading glasses." She showed him the dark rimmed specs.

A wicked curl lifted the corner of his mouth. "I'm envisioning you, out of that suit and in nothing but those glasses. My fantasies include sexy librarians."

Holy crap. Her wolf panted and she barely kept herself in check as her own imagination soared. "We don't have time for your teenage infatuations."

With a low laugh, he escorted her out to the car, the light pressure of his fingers at her elbow sending shivers of want up her spine.

The drive to the first home was made in relative silence and she resolved to do her best. Despite how grief-stricken the family members were, their respect and affection for their Alpha was apparent, and all she had to do was offer her condolences and stand supportively beside him.

It wasn't until the last home they visited that the pattern changed. An attractive female opened the door to them and her attitude was blatantly hostile. Jett bore it stoically as he spoke with her and a small child who gazed at them both in confusion. They weren't offered a seat, instead standing awkwardly just inside the door. The blonde heard them out and there was nothing else to do.

"You had no right sending Trevor," she gritted as she watched them leave.

Jett immediately turned back and held out his hand. "There weren't enough single males to rout the rogues, Marsha. We all had to pitch in."

"This pack doesn't have the reputation so many of the others do, Jett. That's why those rogues are sniffing around. If you set a firmer standard they'd move elsewhere."

"Not true—"

Marsha shut the door on his quiet protest, and River grabbed his hand. "She's hurting and saying things she doesn't mean." Though she wondered about firmer standards...

Squeezing her fingers, he walked her back to the SUV. "Maybe so. In any event, I'll open the pack books for you and have you set up a trust fund for her and the other families. They won't do without."

Being without a loved one couldn't be solved by money, but not having to worry about finances could lift some of the burden. "I can do that."

"My laws aren't as stringent as some, River. That's what Marsha meant. I prefer to view it as being progressive and forward thinking, encouraging pack members to think for themselves when appropriate, but some view it as weakness. That I'm not in control and can be usurped, hence the rogues sniffing around."

She couldn't imagine such a thing. Jett was obviously respected and in charge. And he held to important things, like destiny and claiming... She pursed her lips, still a little shocked that she was coming to accept his assertion of his will without consulting her in the slightest.

They arrived home shortly before one o'clock and were greeted with the smell of something with cheese. River sniffed and looked at Jett.

"I put a pan of food in the oven and set the timer before we left. Some kind of pasta thing."

"You are a good cook."

Her graceful mate shifted awkwardly. "I didn't prepare the meal."

"You have a ton of things in your fridge and freezer. Do you have a housekeeper?"

"No. The single females I..." He made a rueful face before arching a brow.

Understanding crashed over her. She hadn't given his immediate past any thought. As a single wolf, especially an alpha, he would never have lacked for female attention. Her wolf snarled, but she leashed her. Jealousy over something she had no control over was for losers. "What? They rewarded you with ... food?"

Jett's blue eyes widened and then narrowed. He made a big show out of checking his watch. "Upstairs. In our bed. Naked. Move."

Moisture pooled between her legs and her nipples tingled before tightening into hard points as her heat flared. With a composure that belied her inner need, she sauntered toward the stairs, the weight of his stare palpable on her backside. She'd poked the wolf—on purpose—and damned if she wasn't looking forward to the consequences.

Gaining their bedroom, she removed her clothes swiftly but carefully, hanging the jacket and matching skirt with deliberation. Her brain was more in control, the mindless desire buffered, not that she didn't *need*. She needed Jett. She wanted him, and dropping her underwear on the floor, she slipped into their bed, naked as ordered.

"Turned the oven off, sweetheart. But we're on a timetable. My sister will be here shortly. And Tahl." Jett paced through the doorway, his jacket dangling from one long finger, working his shirt buttons open with the other.

River's gaze snagged on the sun-kissed flesh

being revealed. She'd seen him wearing far less, exactly nothing, but her heart thundered and her lower belly hollowed as he tormented her with a slow and deliberate exposure. Casually, she let the sheet slither down the slope of one breast and was rewarded with a quirked brow and a sensuous smile.

"I've unleashed a monster." Jett lost his shirt and wrenched open his slacks in almost the same movement, his silk boxers tented and damp from his huge erection. That garment fell to the floor and he was on the bed in one long step, his eyes glowing wolf-like with golden flecks amongst the blue.

She impulsively placed both hands on his broad chest, the planes of muscle shifting beneath her touch and shoved him backward to sprawl alongside her. Raking her gaze over him, she focused her stare on his cock. She reached a hand to grasp him gently, sliding her palm upward until she could work her thumb over the broad head.

He drew in a quick breath and she quickly looked at his face. It was a mask of desire, his handsome features nearly lupine, and she squeezed harder. The strength of him, an iron rod beneath such soft, supple skin was a marvel, and she leaned forward to trace the pulsing vein on the underside with her tongue.

"Damn it, River." Jett arched into her hand and his cock pulsed beneath her mouth.

Others were due to arrive shortly, she knew it, but he was the Alpha and once in a while they could wait on him. Couldn't they? She explored the heated flesh with her fingers and her tongue, dancing little flicks around the underside of the shaft where it met the mushroom-like head. Jett groaned and when she sucked the corona into her mouth, he said something quite incoherent.

Feeling very much in control, she licked and

sucked with abandon, taking a bit more of him with every bob of her head until he hit the back of her throat. She gagged and swallowed, a spurt of salty liquid easing the way. His big hands fit around the sides of her head, grasping her hair, and tugged her up.

"Enough, sweetheart. Or I'll come down your throat."

Letting him slide free over the curl of her tongue, she blinked languidly at him. "That's okay."

"It won't do anything for your heat."

That was likely true. Her wolf liked his taste and his size but was craving him in a different manner. "Another time."

"Fuck, yes. And you'll tell me who taught you how to give head like that."

He flipped her to her back and loomed, his shoulders bulging with muscle as he braced himself on his hands, his eyes wild with … jealousy?

She wanted that cock inside of her, a molten ache firing between her legs, but a giggle welled up and escaped. He narrowed his stare and she laughed again. "All those romance novels paid off then."

His lips twitched in the next moment. "I'll check out your reading material, sweetheart. There's likely other things you can … practice."

She couldn't think of one as he pushed inside her on a long, slow glide, opening her to accommodate his girth. Without the frenzy of the other times, she felt the exquisite stretch and drag against sensitive tissues and the fit of him against the mouth of her womb. Almost too big, he filled her to the brim. Lifting her legs she wrapped them around his narrow hips and drew him closer. As his wide chest lowered to press against her breasts, she clasped her hands at the back of his neck.

Their connection felt intimate and certain, and

River reveled in that moment.

"Gotta move," Jett muttered, against her temple, and his cock shuttled backward before advancing.

With faster and longer strokes, he fucked her, except it felt a lot more than fucking, and she responded to meet him thrust for thrust. Arching her pelvis into him, his arms wrapped her up tight as he drove her higher. A prickle of energy bloomed high in her channel as his cock swelled impossibly larger and she exploded around him.

"You're squeezing me so hard. So good." He shuddered in her arms and made a guttural sound of deep pleasure.

River set her mouth in the hollow above his collar bone and let her wolf loose to fix her teeth there. Jett tensed and then cursed, his cock tangibly jerking deep inside of her. She licked the tiny wound clean and pressed a kiss on the site. "You're okay," she whispered.

Collapsing to one side of her, Jett raised up on one elbow and stared into her eyes. "More than okay, River. Never more okay."

Wanting his kiss, she parted her lips and he obliged, fitting his mouth to hers in a languorous taste. The sound of a doorbell, followed by a sharp rapping interrupted the magic, and River wondered how long Desiree had been waiting.

On a chuckle, Jett pulled away—and out of her— and reached for his boxers. She managed to keep from reaching for him to prolong the connection. "Go clean up, sweetheart. The rest of the afternoon isn't going to be at all … pleasurable."

She took another minute to surreptitiously watch him yank on a pair of jeans and a blue t-shirt. His fingers patted her mark and his mouth softened. Her heart melted. She was in deep.

****

Desiree was involved in a discussion with Jett when River made it downstairs, once again wearing jeans and a t-shirt. Her hair was damp, but she hadn't wanted to take any more time to dry it. The other she-wolf wore jeans as well, but tightly fitted to display her long legs and tight, curved butt. The button-down shirt, tucked into the jeans, should have looked casual, but snug as it was, it showcased Desi's other assets.

"Sorry I disturbed you." Desiree's tone indicated she was anything but.

"It's fine." Jett gave her a narrow look, and she smiled. "Actually, your timing sucked."

"Oh. Uh, I didn't mean—" The young woman shed some of her confidence and didn't appear quite so distant.

"I told Jett the reasons for my antipathy in helping out the females held by the rogues."

Tilting her head, and casting a glance at Jett, his sister said, "I guess I made it clear how I felt when you backed up."

"You did." River wondered how much to share. "You already know how I feel about single males."

A narrow line appeared between Desi's feathered brows. "Right."

"I thought I had sufficient motive to avoid them, Desiree. Because I believed ... that someone I knew very well had been taken advantage of."

"Like those she-wolves the rogues held?" Desi leaned forward on her chair, beautiful face drawn into worried lines.

"Not to that extent," River admitted. "But it ... marked me and I was afraid I'd be all wrong for those women."

"Oh, River. I get it. I'm sorry. I judged you, and

after I enjoyed meeting you so much. I'll help out and I know Mom will, too. You don't have to worry."

Taking a seat next to her sister-in-law, she shook her head. "Jett explained some things to me. Someday I'll tell you, once I figure out how I could have been so thick."

"You weren't *thick*, sweetheart. You lacked information and you carried some memories that warped your understanding." Jett came to stand beside her and set a possessive hand on her shoulder.

"Regardless, I'll meet with those women. But if you'll have my back I'd appreciate it."

Desiree looked in between them and nodded. "For sure. We should probably get over there pretty quick. We can talk on the way."

Jett checked his watch. "Give it a couple of minutes."

"Why?"

River wanted to do something to distract the young woman and extricate Jett from what was going to be a bad time but felt it wasn't her place. She went with her gut and left him to it.

"There's something you need to know."

"What? What's going on?"

"That's my cue." Tahl strode in from the direction of the foyer. "I let myself in, Jett. I didn't want to disturb you and River."

"You have the code and I don't?" Desiree had repositioned herself in the chair, offering a full view of her voluptuous body, as she teased Tahl. "I suppose as Jett's lieutenant you're entitled."

Fascinated, River watched as the flirtation played out, except Tahl wasn't looking at Desi with anything other than brotherly tolerance. Couldn't the young *woman* see that? *Would* you *have noticed the*

difference before you had a hot alpha on your tail? Or
was she wrong? Was Tahl's reaction rehearsed?

"I've come to say goodbye."

Desi stiffened, all "come hither" looks vanishing.
"Goodbye? Are you going on vacation? In the middle of
this rogue issue? Or are you convinced we're stable?"

Tahl glanced at Jett, who lifted a shoulder. "We
routed them, and the leader is on the run. But it's not a
vacation. Jett's given me permission to leave the pack
and head over to Ashton Leaf's territory. I expect to
stay."

If it had been her, every thought would have been
written on her face, but Desiree was obviously made of
sterner stuff. Shock muted her lovely features, and her
eyes widened, but then she pulled herself together. "Who
is she?"

Tahl didn't prevaricate. "Peyton. Peyton Leaf."

"The Alpha's granddaughter. Right. She... I
remember her." A wide smile graced Desiree's perfect
lips. "Then I suppose there's nothing to say but
congratulations!"

"We aren't there yet," Tahl protested.

"I hope you get what you need, regardless." Desi
rose gracefully to her feet. "It was great you came by
when I was here to say your goodbyes. River and I have
a sad task ahead, so if you'll excuse us?"

River didn't know Tahl at all, but nonplussed
might be the best way to explain his reaction. He opened
his mouth, and then shut it, before shoving a hand
through his thick blond hair. "Right. Sure. I'll let you go
then while I finalize a few things with Jett."

Desiree didn't look at her brother. She slipped her
arm through River's. "I imagine Kris is escorting us?"

"He is." Jett came to kiss River and she felt Desi
stiffen. It was difficult to truly experience the power and

pleasure of his lips on hers when her sister-in-law was obviously hurting. "Kris and another male will look to your safety. I'll see you both later."

Desi didn't respond, and River stepped back. "I'll do my best," she promised.

"All you can do."

He trailed a hand down her back as she and the young shifter moved toward the doorway, and her spine rippled. He trusted her—and Desi—with the meeting ahead of them, and she would definitely do her best, though wished he was coming along.

In respect for Desi's feelings, she lifted a hand to Tahl.

Chapter Eight

A tall form leaned negligently against a dark SUV parked in the drive. At the sight of them, he straightened and opened the back door. "Kris, and you must be River." It wasn't her imagination that he scanned her from head to toe, and Desi put a finger up.

"River, this is Kris. He's on Jett's council, and looks like he's in charge of getting us safely from here to there."

Kris squared his shoulders and kept his gaze on River's face. "Nice to meet you."

"Likewise." She didn't mean it but resolved to reserve judgment until she got to know him better. Besides, she was worried about Desiree and didn't know how they were going to talk with the men in the car.

Another male stepped around the vehicle to nod at them.

"I'm Austin, and you're the Alpha's mate?" He offered his hand and River took it cautiously, relieved when he shook briefly and turned to smile admiringly at Desi. "Kris and I will take you to ... our destination."

"Hi." She waited for her sister-in-law to get in first.

Desiree eased past him, with a flutter of her lashes, but even River could tell her heart wasn't in it. "It's okay, Austin. We don't need the address and we know what's waiting for us."

"That's good then. I was there this morning, but I don't think they're keen on having males around. But they say they're settling in, and they know you're coming. At least that someone's coming from the Alpha."

Settling into the SUV, River risked a glance at

Desi who appeared entranced with the passing scenery as Kris powered away. She gently laid a hand on the other woman's arm and her head whipped around to face her. Desiree's face was set in calm lines, but her eyes reflected the torment within. She blinked, and the pain vanished.

Arching a brow, Desi said, "We'll soon be there." Lowering her voice, River replied, "Are you—" "Not now." River heard, *not ever*. Okay then. She had zero experience with the heartbreak of others and hoped Desi's mother did. As if by mutual accord, the rest of the drive continued in silence until they drew up in front of a large, two-story house with a beautifully landscaped yard.

"Nine bedrooms and about half as many baths. It's the biggest place we could find other than a dormitory at the University in the city. This is more private and easily defended. We call it the Sanctuary." Austin stepped out and pulled open the back door.

"Defended?" River climbed out and Desi followed. They stood together, staring at the house. There was no sign of life.

"We don't know enough about these women. Jett wants them safe and protected until they move on or stay. You'll figure out if they need counseling or whatever. Anything else. But there's a chance they might be more … connected to a rogue than we know."

Her knees weakened. These female shifters had likely been brutalized—mistreated at best—and one or more might have been claimed. Could that be a good thing or… There was a whole lot more to deal with than even the resettlement issues, and she supposed she would learn as she went.

"No time like the present," Desi mumbled and motioned River ahead with a flick of her hand.

She rang the bell and tried out a few greetings in her head. The males took a position on the porch out of sight, their faces grim. At length, a tall, red-haired she-wolf cautiously opened the door.

"I'm River Fortuna. The Alpha's mate. This is his sister, Desiree." She didn't know Desi's last name and faltered.

"Desiree Bolton. May we come in?"

"Of course. I'm Moira." She didn't volunteer her last name and River made a mental note to determine who all these women were, in order to track down their packs. Although perhaps they didn't wish for anyone to know... They walked behind Moira down a long hallway and entered a great room that probably looked out over the forest—if the drapes weren't closed tightly.

Over a dozen women gathered inside. A television flickered in the corner, and some of them held books on their laps, but the rest simply sat. Without exception, all of them were pale and gaunt. River's heart dropped to her feet. She knew if she looked closer, she'd see the residual marks of injuries, and she really didn't want to look in their eyes.

"Is everyone here?"

"A few are upstairs and won't come out of their rooms."

"Okay. I have some things I'd like to say here first, and I'll go up and talk with the others individually?" Moira seemed to be in charge, although she looked fatigued and shaken.

Nodding, the redhead pointed to an empty chair. River took it and Desiree sank down at her feet. Introducing them, she tried to make eye contact with everyone and asked their names. Too many to remember. Sandra, Louise, Tina, Bettina, Christine, Barbra, the list went on, all delivered in similar listless tones.

"I'll ask Moira to make a list of everyone, but for now, we'll leave it at first names."

"We lost our packs." Tina, she thought it was, made the comment.

"Who said?"

"The Regent. He told us they wouldn't want us back."

"We'll see. I'm not inclined to take a rogue's word."

"We're rogue."

"You're not unless you chose to leave."

Moira said, "None of us down here chose. A couple upstairs did, lured away by a handsome face. They're pretty upset because their males are either dead or on the road."

So she and Desi would indeed face some acrimony, but there was nothing else to do but face it. "If you didn't choose, then you're not rogue. And if your packs don't... That is, if you can't return, you're welcome here."

Slowly, using her analytical skills, because they served much better here than her emotions, which were all over the map, River coaxed information from those present and sketched out an overall plan. Desi filled them in on the pack, seeing as she was much more familiar.

"We'll provide you with a therapist, and continuing medical care." Some of them accepted but others were reticent. Again, time would tell.

Leaving them to consider the options, feeling a taste of hope in the air, she climbed the stairs. There were four women huddled in separate rooms. Three refused to even look up and pretended not to hear anything she and Desi said. They would be the ones connected to the single males.

"Were you claimed?" she asked each one. That

elicited a response. An adamant shake of the head accompanied a hostile glare in each case. The fourth woman, Denise, proved to be the exception.

She didn't respond at all, lying on her bed with her face turned to the wall. But her shoulders shook with sobs and River cautiously approached. "Will you tell me his name? We might be able to determine his whereabouts."

When Denise remained mute, she said, "If you change your mind, tell Moira. She can call me, or give you my number."

Drained, she preceded Desiree downstairs where Moira waited.

"I made up that list. For the ones upstairs too, though I don't know..."

"Thanks. We'll figure it out from here. You're kinda the leader of them."

"More like a sorority mother of a dysfunctional group of women. Dysfunctional women." The redhead tried to smile but hiccupped on a sob.

"We'll arrange for someone to come here and see you, individually. Perhaps group therapy," offered Desi.

"Not so sure that works when the other members of the group were front and center for most of what happened."

Or it could mean that there'd be no hiding or denial, thought River, having made some recent revelations herself. But she said nothing. That would be up to the therapist.

****

Moira locked up behind them, the sound of the deadbolt snapping in the clear afternoon air. Austin went ahead to once again open the vehicle and Kris brought up the rear. River didn't like having the male behind her and hurried to get inside the SUV, silently berating herself for over-reacting.

"That went better than I expected." Desiree leaned her head back and closed her eyes. "Those poor women."

"They're in bad straits," River agreed. She considered the sheets of paper folded in her hand. "Once we find out where their packs stand, especially on the ones who went willingly, we'll know how to proceed. Although we'll send someone over to talk with them regardless."

"The pack has a couple of shifter-friendly therapists."

"Really?" She didn't think her old pack had any, but then she'd avoided learning too much about anyone there.

"What about Denise?"

That was troubling. "I don't know. I'll talk to Jett."

"Atta girl."

"What?"

Desi turned her head and smiled. "You've already learned when to handle things yourself and when to ask your mate."

Was that what it was? River figured she simply knew her own limitations but didn't enlighten the other woman. "We have to work it out. Those females are going to take a long time to heal." *If ever.* "Kris, is there any chance of any of those rogues finding those women?"

"No. No one followed us, and we have someone watching the place. The women have no way of communicating with the outside. No phone or internet access. Moira knows she can signal our guys if she needs anything."

"Right."

"Do you want us to drop you at your house, Desiree?" Kris asked.

"Yes. Unless you need me for something else, River?"

She tried to read the other woman's face but detected nothing but calm resolve. Desi wasn't open to talking about herself, at least not yet. "If Jett knows who to call for therapy for the women, I'm good. But I'd like to spend more time with you."

"Another time." Desi's smile nearly took the sting out of the rejection, and in truth, River didn't take it personally. She knew what it was like to be self-reliant and Jett's mother would be home in the next day or so.

"Okay. I'll call you."

"Sure."

Desiree lived in a much smaller house than Jett's, with her mother, but the place had charm and character. It reminded River of an old English cottage. She hoped Desi would invite her over sooner than later. "See you."

Nothing in the way her sister-in-law moved indicated that she'd received a blow to her self-esteem, and worse, her heart, followed by a sad and depressing visit to a house full of abused women. She stepped gracefully to the house with a wave and disappeared inside. River heard Austin sigh and looked to see him watching Desiree's progress with intent.

They pulled away and it occurred that she was alone with two single wolves. Austin didn't bother her at all, but Kris wasn't as easy to share space with, and she wondered why that was. Taking out her cell, she considered calling Jett then decided to wait until she saw him. There was no need for the tether of a phone call.

His vehicle wasn't in the driveway, and she experienced a keen sense of loss, once she identified the hollowness in her belly and tightness in her throat. The males escorted her to the door and she entered the code.

"I'll wait with you, River," Kris announced. "Austin has other things to take care of."

Austin smiled, his dark eyes crinkling at the corners, and she realized he was older than her first appeared. "I hope to see you soon."

"Likewise." And she meant it.

Kris sauntered toward the kitchen as if familiar with the house, and she supposed he was. But it was her home, and her right to offer anything. "Would you like something to drink?"

He slowed and stopped. "Oh. Sorry. I'm used to organizing things at the council meetings. I was going to get us a couple of beers."

"I don't drink beer." *And I shouldn't be drinking anything alcoholic right now, for more reasons than one.* "I'll make tea and get you a beer. You can take a seat in the living room."

With a slight smile, he headed that way. "Thanks."

Setting the kettle to boil, she found a tea to her liking and reached for her cell. It was silenced, out of respect for the women she had gone to see, and she checked the screen. Jett had left her a text, citing a matter to take care of and would see her soon. She checked the end of the message for an emoticon, flinching at her disappointment when there wasn't one. *Silly, romantic female.*

Carrying her mug and a bottle of beer with a glass crammed over the neck, she headed to where Kris presumably waited. The male was sprawled over the end of the couch, one arm stretched out along the back, long legs cramped by the placement of the coffee table. River set his beer down and took a chair as far from him as she could manage.

"Thanks." He leaned to free the glass and set it aside, taking a swig directly from the bottle. "Sounds like you did a nice job with those females," he complimented.

"It was more Desi than me." She wished Jett would soon get home. Her wolf was restless and she too craved what he could give her. Her heat was waning, but he'd said something about the many times in between...

"Jett figured you'd do right by them and, as usual, he knows what he's talking about." Kris ignored her deprecating comment and gave her an admiring glance that swept from head to toe. "We knew he'd pick the right mate."

"You're all very loyal."

"He demands loyalty. More like commands it. He doesn't ask anyone to do anything he wouldn't and we follow him willingly. It doesn't hurt that he surrounds himself with wolves who know what they're doing."

How was it that Kris could compliment both Jett and the other council members yet come across as being such an egotist? River decided she didn't much like him. Maybe if she got busy in the kitchen she could put a lid on her need for Jett. She placed her tea on a coaster to make her way there. "I'm going to make something to eat for me and Jett. Can I fix you anything?"

"Sure." He leaned into her space and sniffed. Appalled at his rudeness, she stepped back, and Kris had the grace to look sheepish. "Sorry. It's your heat. Makes the single wolves crazy."

Cheeks flaming, she crossed her arms over her breasts. "You're being offensive. Better you leave."

His eyebrows shot up and he blinked. "What? Shit, River. I guess your pack is more formal. Again, I apologize, but I think we can put aside those formalities. I mean, there's no need for them between us."

"What are you talking about?"

"I'm one of the single males Jett can call upon to assuage your mating heat. He and I have helped others in the past with their mates. Kind of the go-to guys." He winked.

Her first instinct was to flee. But she'd done enough running. If her mate had made arrangements without talking to her about it, she was going to hurt him in painful and creative ways. For once her wolf was in total agreement, snarling at the thought of Kris touching her. "What makes you think we require your assistance?"

"I guess I don't. Not exactly. But I asked him if he'd share you and he said—" Kris furrowed his brow. "I don't remember what he said, but you're still in heat so I assumed."

"I'm not talking to you about this." She invaded Kris's space this time and poked him in the chest. "It's between Jett and me. I don't need any single males in my bed."

"*Our* bed." Jett vibrated in the doorway. A big man, he'd never deliberately used his size to intimidate her, but wrath fairly emanated from every pore. River hurried over to him, blissfully aware she was totally safe. He tucked her alongside him and some of the tension bled off.

Kris piped up, "Hey. I was just explaining to River—"

"That you wanted to offer assistance?"

"Right. Exactly." Kris's face creased in puzzlement.

"Did I request it?"

"Uh, no."

"Then what the fuck are you doing offering it?"

The other male's face tightened in shock. He shook his head, and then bowed it, setting a fist over his heart. "Presuming. My deepest apologies."

River watched Kris stride past. He didn't look at either of them, merely hustled out the door. It shut quietly, a marked contrast to the screaming testosterone in the room. Then Jett squeezed her. "That wolf and I are having a serious fucking discussion in the near future. You okay?"

"I am. Better than you'd have been if you'd actually thought to share me with that man."

Nuzzling her hair, he replied, "I'd have to sleep with one eye open for the rest of my life." He paused and held her closer. "You're still in heat."

"Some. But mostly thinking about you and what you promised."

He stared into her eyes. "Were you?"

"Weren't you?"

"Wench."

"I shouldn't even be thinking about it," she nearly whispered. "Not when there's so much pain around us."

"Sex—procreation—always increases when there's a tragedy, sweetheart. I think it's a way of celebrating life, understanding that we are still around when others aren't." He leaned down to take her lips and the kiss fired up her waning heat, making her wolf howl.

Her feet barely touched the stairs as Jett spirited her up them.

****

She relaxed on her belly, occasionally twitching as Jett traced her spine with a rough fingertip from nape to the small of her back, over and over.

"Your skin is like silk."

"Umm."

"And your ass is perfect." He cupped first one buttock then the other, and she squirmed.

A sharp spank pulled her completely out of her contented drowse and she flounced onto her side to stare at him. "Ow! What was that for?"

"I love the way your skin pinks when I smack it."

That comment shouldn't have stoked her desire, but coupled with the sensuous timbre in his voice and the naked lust in his eyes, she felt the first stirrings of a physical response. "You'll have to find something else to love then because you are not spanking me again."

"Made an impression, did it?"

"You know it did. I went off on you because of it. I'm not letting you bully me."

Jett frowned. "A correction isn't bullying. Now that I've come to know you better, I can see there was another way to deal with you breaking pack law, though." He took her hand.

She melted. This male wasn't too proud to own his mistakes. She'd better own hers. "I don't know if talking to me about it would have had such an impact. At least not until I understood about the heat issue."

He yanked her to his chest and kissed her hair. "Such a good girl."

"Not a girl," she mumbled against his damp skin, noting that his cock was once again up for the challenge, pulsing against her abdomen.

"An endearment." He held her closer.

"Okay, snuggle buns."

He shook with laughter, the sound rumbling against her cheek. "Sweetheart it is. I notice you don't object to that."

"So the therapists will be there tomorrow morning?" She figured they needed to pay attention to the pack.

"Both of them. They put this as a priority. And I'll reach out to the packs shortly. Thank you for going this morning, sweetheart."

"It's my role, Jett. And I'm glad I did, regardless.

Desi was kind and supportive too."

He hitched to sit against the headboard, easing her along with him. She looked up at him, his face worried and eyes somber. "How was my sister? She took Tahl's news better than I could have hoped. I guess he's just one of many Desi is interested in."

"She was gutted."

"What? Shocked, maybe and surprised. I mean, we'll all miss Tahl—"

"Heartbroken might cover it, but she doesn't want anyone to see it, especially him. She has her pride."

"Shit. My mother is going to want to kill him."

"I'm not sure she'll even let on to your mom. I mean, I don't know how close they are, but it feels as though Desi ... shut down. She probably needs some time. Not that I'm particularly wise in the nuances of romance."

"You're getting better," he teased, again cupping her ass.

Somehow ignoring the weight of his big hand against her skin, all five digits spanning her buttock and creating spirals of awareness to wreak havoc on her senses, River said, "Well, I suppose I have a lot of catching up to do. Kris seems to be in awe of your exploits."

Groaning, he tipped his head back and screwed his eyes shut. "I'd hoped you missed that part of the conversation."

"Kinda hard to do so, when you bragged about your prowess already. And you pointed out that you know about who has needed assistance, being the Alpha and all. The single Alpha."

He rolled her under him with that unerring ability to position her exactly as he needed. Caged by his arms and trapped beneath his bulk, she never felt safer. He rested his forehead against hers, his eyes crossing comically. "We'll leave that in the past too, River. There'll be no other woman in my bed but you."

The press of his cock against her core erased any hint of her teasing as it worked past the stricture of her entrance and deep inside. She should tell him there'd be no other man for her but speaking became too much of an effort compared to simply feeling, and she gave in to his skilled possession.

Chapter Nine

Jett's mother, Marlene, was nothing like what River expected. Jett and Desiree were both tall, well-built individuals, and the pictures of his other sister confirmed she was the same. Marlene wasn't even as tall as River, and comfortably plump accurately described her. Her blonde hair was streaked with silver and she wore it in a casual twist on her neck.

A stylish tunic top over capris and a pair of flat sandals completed her ensemble, another sop to fashion being some nice earrings and bangles adorning her left wrist. A pair of sun glasses sat atop her head.

But the eyes were all Jett, Desi, and Lizbeth. Those orbs were a pale, icy blue, and Marlene studied her thoroughly with those familial eyes as Jett presented her.

"She's perfect, son."

River somehow stayed upright. The relief that his mom approved of her was staggering, not that anyone or anything messed with a bond. But it was important to her that her mother-in-law liked her. For Jett's sake. She gave Marlene her best smile.

"You've been thrown in the deep end, I hear."

"It's been interesting." Aware that Marlene indeed harbored no wolf, she strained to determine what other paranormal entity favored the older woman.

"Come and sit with me. We'll get to know one another."

"Sure." With a glance at Jett, she followed Marlene.

"I'll be in my office."

She turned on her heel and went to him, going up on tip toe to offer her lips. He obliged, stealing her breath, and his lids lowered at her reaction. "Can't bear to be away from me for even a few minutes."

It was true, and his teasing might have stung, but she knew he felt the same. "Come join us when you're finished."

"I won't leave you alone with her for too long." He released her and patted her backside. That man and her ass.

Marlene was installed in one of the club chairs, her feet tucked up beneath her. Her smile was tolerant and satisfied. "Every heat is the same, River. It binds ever stronger." The pleased look dimmed. "It can also make the pair vulnerable, of course."

Wondering if Jett had told Marlene about River's preconceived notion of being claimed, she hesitated to respond. "It subsides during pregnancy though."

"Eh? Oh, right. It does, a blessing in some respects, considering you're at the beck and call of the baby, even before it's born. Shifter pregnancies can be intense."

"You've had three."

"Four, actually. Frederick and I lost one between Lizbeth and Desiree. And Jett was an easy carry."

Desperately wanting to ask, River nevertheless bit her tongue. "Did you want something? Tea? Coffee?"

"Later, thanks. For now, I'd like to hear about your family. And Jericho's pack."

River filled her in, and Marlene made the appropriate noises at the correct moments to support how intently she appeared to listen. "I'm sorry you lost your mother so young. I hope you and I can spend time together."

"I'd like that." She meant it, sensing nothing but kindness in the older woman, along with something a little strange, but not nasty.

"I have Fae blood. My relationship with Jericho triggered the gene, or so our doctors think. We simply don't have enough information to figure it all out. Jett is the product of a chance mating, and he'll carry it too. The gene. Are you okay with that?"

"I hadn't considered it. I mean, I didn't know much about you—and Jericho. You don't think it will hurt our pups?" Her hand pressed involuntarily against her belly.

"Extremely doubtful," Marlene said briskly, "but they could develop quicker or have some additional skills. You should know to expect it."

"That would be all right."

"We should probably go make some refreshments, honey. I can tell we have lots more to talk about. And I have lots to tell you about the man who claimed you. About forty years' worth."

They settled in the kitchen and conversed over cold drinks while Marlene regaled her with stories about Jett's childhood. River knew she skipped over some of the more difficult times, seeing as she was beginning to read the other woman's nonverbal cues pretty well. Nothing much was said about Jericho, although she gained the impression that the affair was intense, and if Marlene had been a shifter, things would have turned out different. But she spoke very fondly of her deceased husband as well.

"What do you do, Marlene? I know Desi said you had a business."

"I own a women's clothing boutique in town. I was on a buyer's trip when Desiree called about the incident with the rogues. She said you had things under control, you and Jett, but how can I help?"

"There are four women I expect will require extra support because I doubt their packs will take them back.

Or that they'll want to return. Maybe we can go and see them once the therapists have some time to work."

"Of course. And perhaps you'll have time to come to the shop. Desi said you wanted to revamp your wardrobe."

"I do. I have some suitable stuff but nothing nice for casual. And my underwear is pretty basic." She flushed and Marlene laughed.

"Well, you'll be coming to the right place. I have everything a woman might want."

"I'll come as soon as possible."

Sipping at her drink, Marlene asked, "Do you know what's up with my daughter?"

"Uh, I don't know if... I mean, best she talk to you?"

"Tahl went to the Dawnfall clan, Mom." Jett strode in and helped himself to a cookie. "He told Desi personally, and I thought she wasn't bothered, but River thinks differently."

River stared at her hands and wished she knew what to say.

"Oh, dear. She'll be devastated, and denying it every inch of the way. I suppose it's a female?" Marlene's voice was pained.

"Ashton's granddaughter. I don't remember her very well."

"She was an annoying, pretentious twit when they were here, but if Tahl can't see that I suppose there's nothing to be done."

"Desiree can stand to grow up a little, too, Mom. I'm sorry she was hurt, but Tahl didn't view things the same way."

"Then he was blind. But that's my mother side talking. Or the human one. Even with my ability to fit in with shifters I can't always comprehend this claiming business. The females being slaves to their heat and requiring a male. I appreciate your tolerance in regard to women being allowed to exhibit their interest prior to coming into heat."

"Mom." River jumped at the terse tone. Jett was glaring at his parent.

"I know. Pack history. Destiny. All of that. You're fortunate River was both willing and suitable."

River opened her mouth, but Jett cut her off.

"We're fated mates, Mom. At least to judge by the connection we're developing. River will be finishing my sentences in no time."

"And you'll be reading my mind," she said sweetly.

Marlene burst into laughter. "Maybe not such a slave, then. Even better. You've had things your way for too long, son."

"I can't wait until Desi and Lizbeth join forces with you against me," he grumbled.

Changing the subject, River said, "When's a good time for me to see your mom's boutique?"

"Tomorrow, if you can finalize the paperwork for the families of the wolves we lost. I'd like to get that done as soon as possible. Before we work out what transpires for the females the rogues took."

"I'm going to visit those families today, after I leave here," Marlene said. "You come by before lunch tomorrow and we'll have a bite to eat, and then I'll turn you loose in the boutique. Desi will probably come too. It'll be good for her—in case she wants to talk."

"I'll drop you off, sweetheart, and if I can't come for you when you're finished, Austin will pick you up. I don't anticipate any trouble, but until I'm certain, I don't want you wandering around by yourself."

It was stupid to argue, although Jett was being all

alpha male, so she nodded. "I get it."

Marlene tucked a few strands of wayward hair back into its twist and headed out. "I loved meeting you and look forward to lunch tomorrow. Get some rest, honey. Although the way my son is watching you, I don't think that's on his agenda."

It was on hers, because she was drained of energy. It had been a momentous couple or three days. She was too tired to even blush at her mother-in-law's suggestive comment. "I'll be there before noon."

Enveloped in a warm hug, River sniffed the floral bouquet Marlene exuded and soaked in the kindness. Lizbeth lived in a different pack, but hopefully she'd get along with her as well, when they came to meet. Having Cass come to visit would make everything perfect, and she resolved to call her sister as soon as they were alone.

Jett set his arm around her shoulders as they walked his mother to the door. She leaned into him. "I'd like to call Cass."

"Absolutely. Come find me when you're finished and we'll put dinner together."

Free to talk and share anything and everything, she headed to their room and placed the call. She reached her sister and was predictably overwhelmed by the girl's emotional response. But Cass accepted the news that River had been claimed—not that there was a time reference made—and confided that their father already knew. Apparently Jett had notified Jericho who in turn advised Reginald. Despite her increasing connection to her mate, the paternalism grated.

"When can I visit?" Cass was bubbling with excitement. "Is your place nice? Are there lots of shifters my age?"

Her sister didn't know about the action taken against the rogues, and didn't need to hear about the women rescued from them. River didn't want her here until she was certain it was safe, or as safe as it could be. "I need a little time with Jett, Cass. This is all new for us." Well, for her, mostly.

"Of course. Oh, River, I'm happy for you. You sound good. You are, aren't you? Even if you wanted a different life?"

"I'm happy. Even content." It was astonishing how much she'd changed and how well she'd adapted, considering she'd longed to escape this life. It was reflected in her sincere response.

They exchanged promises to call more often, and Cass was satisfied, knowing a visit to her sister was in the near future.

River ran down the stairs to find Jett, vaguely aware of hearing people coming and going while she was on the phone. She walked into his office and stumbled to a halt, her upper body leaning against the sudden stop until she gained her balance. Jett was lounging back in his chair. She hear him chuckling, although the voluptuous figure of the she-wolf sitting on the edge of his desk blocked her view.

The female turned, her movement thrusting out an extremely well-endowed chest. Two finely plucked brows on a heavily made up face rose in response to seeing her.

Jett stood, looming over the other woman. "River. Come and meet Tawny."

Tawny. Of course. If not Tawny, it could have been Bambi. Shocked at her malicious reaction, River faked a wide smile and forced her feet to move. "Hey. Nice to meet you."

Tawny didn't offer an extravagantly manicured hand, the nails curved like talons, and neither did she smile. Instead, she gave River the once over and sniffed.

"I heard Jett claimed a mate." Her tone said she didn't think much of his choice, as she swung a long, bare leg. Her skirt barely covered her crotch, so there was lots of leg to expose.

River locked her stare on Jett and willed him to come to her. Maybe there was something to his belief in fated mates, because he stepped around the siren displayed on his desk and moved to River.

Tucking against his side, she felt the familiar weight of his arm wrapping around her, and nodded at Tawny. "You heard correctly. Were you *one* of the females who kept his fridge stocked?"

Jett tensed but said nothing, while the other woman paled, her blush standing out in two ragged patches high on her cheeks.

"I ... I suppose so."

"He ate well by the look of things, and I appreciate he was taken care of."

Tawny slithered to the floor, her stilettos clacking on the hardwood. She was sex on a stick. River willingly admitted it, and her mate obviously thought the same way—before. There had been no hint of sexual interest until his body came into contact with River's. Her wolf remained alert, attention focused on the interloper, but becoming distracted by Jett's proximity.

"We're about to make dinner, if you'd like to stay?" She gave Tawny her most innocent, sweet look and the other woman flinched.

"I can't. I stopped by with my sister and brother to see Jett and give him my regards. And to meet you, of course."

"Of course. I imagine we'll be seeing a lot of one another, as I'm, you know, the Alpha's mate."

"Of course." Tawny wasn't pleased but granted the match to River. "I'll just head out. My ride will be waiting anyhow."

She sashayed past them, casting a look at Jett, but he was staring at River. She slipped from under his arm and ensured the other woman had left, and then dead bolted the door behind her.

"Tawny is—"

"I know what she is, Jett. I think you mentioned dinner?"

A panty-melting smile was bestowed on her. "I made a good choice, sweetheart. You exceed all expectations."

"Then you'd better give some thought to exceeding mine."

Jett sputtered, or whatever an alpha male did when challenged, and she hustled to the kitchen. Hard on her heels, he caught her up and lifted her to sit on the island. Setting a big hand on either side of her hips, he regarded her seriously, one corner of his chiseled mouth quirking upward. "Point taken. Tawny doesn't have boundaries. But as Alpha—and your mate—that'll be up to me to enforce some."

"That's a good thing, because it looks as though I'll have enough to do in my new role without dealing with your many exes."

Stepping between her knees, he spread her thighs wide, the counter a perfect height to allow him to press his engorged cock against her core. "We could postpone dinner."

"Uh uh." She was hungry and believed she could exert some will power over her heat. "Feed me. First."

"Your heat is on the wane. Do you think you're pregnant?"

"Part of me hopes not, because I'd like some time to settle in. Get to know you and your family and the pack better, without dealing with being pregnant," she admitted. "On the other hand, I'd rather not go into heat again in a month."

Nuzzling along her neck, he murmured, "It hasn't been so bad."

"Not, too bad." She managed to keep any hint of humor from her voice, and succeeded, because Jett lifted his head, eyes full of challenge.

"Wench."

She touched his cheek, marking the stubble that already made itself known. Teasing could be fun—and intimate. "Feed me."

Chapter Ten

River settled in over the next several days, busy with reviewing the pack's financial affairs and ensuring she carried out all the necessary settlements for the families of the lost males. Her trip to Marlene's boutique was an enjoyable experience, with Desi making excellent suggestions as to the items that suited her best and made the most of her shape and size.

Her sister-in-law presented as the same happy, enthusiastic young woman she had met her first day arriving in Jett's home. River watched the other female when she thought Desi wasn't looking, and couldn't see any lingering effects from what had to be a betrayal by Tahl—at least in Desiree's eyes. She flirted with Austin and the human waiter at lunch and gave other males speculative and appreciative glances.

River might have concluded that the other woman had bounced back from her obsession with Tahl, except his name never once passed her lips, not even in conversations with others who inquired about his whereabouts. Desi deferred to others, who shared the news. At a loss, River left it alone.

Desi had an online business that included selling merchandise from her mother's boutique as well as several other shifters in the pack. She saw it as cornering the market, and with her skills, she did well, and again requested River's help in learning to budget her income.

"I like working from home and making my own hours. It gives me time to do other things when I'm interested," she confided. "And I like being my own boss. I just need to learn to live within a budget."

River was happy to help and agreed to give Marlene's books a look too. It felt as though she was part of a family—a normal, happy family—and she couldn't wait for Cass to visit.

Jett was busy leading the pack, involved in meetings and spending a great deal of time on the phone. Of grave importance was the resettlement of the rescued females and progress was being made, both on his side and the part of the therapists. He always made time for her and despite the fact her heat had abated—with no pregnancy—she discovered what he'd referenced as all the other times in between heat cycles.

The sex they partook in wasn't the driven, mindless assuaging of her biological need, but rather of a fun and enjoyable nature. She was an equal participant and even instigated the loving.

"Hey. Where'd you go?" Her mate waved a hand in front of her face as she became adrift in her thoughts and lost the thread of their conversation. He leaned against the island, watching her with a small smile softening his lips.

"Just thinking about sex." She didn't even blush, and thoroughly appreciated the slight shock her frank words elicited, as Jett's eyes widened before a brow quirked.

"Where did my resistant little shifter go? The one who was horrified to even hear the word mentioned, let alone think about participating."

"Who said I was thinking about sex with you?"

Cats pounced, foxes too, but wolves? For sure, wolves. Jett's blue eyes glinted gold as he crossed the room in two effortless strides to throw her over his shoulder. He smacked her buttocks the entire way up the stairs as she laughed and flailed ineffectually at *his* fine ass.

The slight sting on her skin beneath the barrier of denim heated her core, not that she was going to let on.

River Fortuna drew the line at spanking—any kind of spanking, though the spirit of this particular paddling was acceptable... Especially when he rubbed his target and the warmth spread further in an indescribable but pleasurable fashion.

Their clothing fell away with the dint of long practice, and she indulged herself with a long look at her mate's splendid physique. Wide shoulders with smoothly muscled biceps and forearms, a broad chest sprinkled with just enough dark hair, an etched six pack... She knew how firm and round his ass was, having had her hands on it often enough, and how long and strong his legs were. As for his cock... Thick and as a perfect of the rest of him, with a wide, soft cap crowning the silky hardness, now dark and beaded with moisture.

"I want to look at your sweet ass as I take you, River." The low timbre in his tone vibrated in her core, and she willingly turned onto her belly, coming up onto her knees. She'd thrown modesty—and any inkling of unworthiness—to the wind, likely by the fourth or fifth time Jett had taken her. He obviously liked what he saw, so why hide from him?

Nipping her shoulders and down the length of her spine, his warm breath washed over her and made her impatient. She wiggled her buttocks against the thrust of his erection and he palmed one flank. "After that remark downstairs, sweetheart, I think I'll make you wait. Just so you're certain who you're having sex with."

"I do! I swear." She wanted the pleasure he always brought her, able to savor and prolong the experience. "Please, Jett."

"Ah, begging." He licked a particularly sensitive spot and inserted a knee between her thighs to widen her stance. "That's a sweet sound."

"C'mon. Please?" Unable to do more than squirm

and shift her weight a little, she whined.

A long finger teased down the crevice of her ass and between her folds to circle around her entrance. As hard as she tried to impale herself on it, she failed as he trailed upward to smear the wetness on her clit. "Argh."

"What's that? How many languages do you speak?"

A dark fantasy of tying *him* to the bed while he slept then teasing him until he shifted, kept her from retorting. Instead, she pleaded again—in English.

He rewarded her with several feather light rubs that made her tingle and begin to reach for an orgasm, before backing off to insert that finger inside, working it in and out against her clenching walls as she tried to match the rhythm.

"You're so wet for me. Me, River."

"You," she agreed. Surely he knew it was only him she thought about? "Only you."

He replaced his finger with the broad head of his cock and pushed the tip inside. River froze and waited for that first full thrust, the one that she'd come to crave as he filled her. Instead, his wet finger pressed gently on her puckered star, making her start.

"I won't hurt you, sweetheart. Can you relax?"

Uh, probably not. She tensed to keep him out, but the broad pad of his digit worked inside the tightness. "Jett?"

"Does it hurt?"

It didn't. It was uncomfortable, sort of, and something else … something different and not totally unwelcome. "No. But—"

Coated her natural lubricant, his finger delved deeper and a jangling sensation caused her pussy to draw up and his cock slipped in further. She sucked in a deep breath against the pillow and tried to process the foreign impression, even as Jett worked an arm beneath her to hold her steady. His large cock made forays forward and back, filling her up as always, but his finger in her ass made him feel even bigger.

Was he wiggling that finger? Twisting it? The forbidden touch didn't mean it felt horrible, in fact, she was being carried along on a myriad of sensations. Unable to catalog them, she surrendered to the magic Jett was wreaking on her senses and burst apart as nerve endings beyond her control fizzled and popped.

"Fuck, sweetheart. You're—" Whatever she was, it was lost as Jett climaxed on a drawn-out groan, his weight dropping over her. His hot seed bathed her channel and prolonged her orgasm.

Panting, she whimpered as he carefully withdrew from her bottom hole, and then from her pussy. Her heart thundered several beats before beginning to slow and the spots behind her eyelids diminished.

"Just imagine how hard you'd come with my cock in there, and your clit stimulated." Jett nuzzled her temple before climbing off the bed. She simply lay there, trying to decide if she could even entertain the possibility.

She clenched and detected no residual discomfort, but his finger and his cock differentiated in size— considerably. Definitely not.

Water ran in the attached bath and she straightened her legs, wincing at the pins and needles. He was at her side in an instant, smoothing his big, roughened palms along her limbs to work out the kinks. Kinks. As he drew a warmth cloth between her thighs, she blinked up at him. "How kinky are you?"

His brows climbed toward his hairline. "As kinky as you'd like me to be."

She hadn't forgotten his idle comment about

tying her to the bed. It didn't frighten her now, but she still wasn't sure... Brightening, her dark fantasy resurfaced. There was nothing to say that two couldn't play.

"What was that look about?" He regarded her with interest. How could such icy-blue eyes hold such warmth?

"I was thinking about tying you up."

He tossed the cloth on the floor and gathered her against him. "I'd trust you to do that, sweetheart. Do you trust me?"

"I do. Though maybe not your ... penis in my backside."

"Did my finger hurt? During?"

"No. But there's a difference in size."

He chuckled, his sweat-damp chest pressing harder against her. "I hope so. But I'd make sure you were ready to take me, you know. I understand there's some pressure and a bit of discomfort even so, but the experience is worth it."

"You *understand*?" He was spoiling the glow.

"Sorry. I'm trying to reassure you is all."

"Uh huh. And talk me into it because you like it."

Hauling her up, he sat her on his lap and looked in her eyes. "I do like it. I won't lie. But if it's not for you, I'm good without it. Promise."

"We'll see," she concluded. "Now, tell me about your other ... interests."

"How about I surprise you?"

"I suppose." She relaxed against him, content to rest and recover and to savor the closeness. Anticipation had its perks.

Besides the intense physical draw, she trusted him and felt safe, the foundation for a far deeper connection. Jett had never said the words, but if what she felt was love, she believed he felt it too. She wasn't going to consider her reaction should he consider them no more than mates, if a fated pair. The casual conversation she'd had with Marlene confirmed the rarity of such a claiming—and the sobering fact that an intense emotional connection didn't necessarily accompany it.

"I'm falling in love with you." It was surprisingly easy to say because it felt so right and she knew he'd understand.

His hand faltered in the stroking of her hair before resuming the soothing motion. A beat of silence passed, then another, and her heart lurched. She desperately wanted to look at his face but was equally afraid of what she might read there. How could she have drawn such a wrong conclusion?

He saved her the trouble. "You honor me, River. Our connection grows stronger each and every day. You mean a great deal to me, and as my fated mate, I can only imagine how our bond will intensify."

She borrowed a page from Desiree's book without a thought. Somehow remaining relaxed and managing her breathing, she hung onto her pride with her fingernails. If her sister-in-law had withstood this body blow, then River would as well. When she was certain she could trust her voice, she replied, "I can only imagine, as well."

Jett set her away from him and tipped her head up with a gentle finger beneath her chin. "You okay?"

"Yes." She willed a smile to twist her lips and gave him what she desperately hoped was a calm and unaffected look. He leaned to kiss her and she turned to catch it on her cheek, slipping off his lap. "Bathroom."

****

He'd fucked up. Royally. He should have responded in the same vein. What would be the harm?

He did care a great deal for River. She was his bonded mate and likely his fated one. All the signals were there. He could have told her loved her back and how would she have known any different? Except he couldn't lie to her. He stared at the bathroom door and wondered if he should follow her. And say what?

Jett had simply never thought about being in love. His mother hadn't loved Jericho, and her relationship with Frederick had been that of a mated she-wolf. And while she had lavished maternal love and attention on Jett whenever she'd been allowed time with him, that certainly wasn't the kind of love River was suggesting. Nor was the affection he bore his sisters.

He considered other relationships within the pack and conceded that some of them had blossomed into more than a claiming, witness how distraught Marsha was over the loss of her mate. But many were but a suitable match imbued with respect and affection that withstood the test of time.

Of all the women he'd been with, the physical lure had been the mainstay, and even that had been fleeting and interchangeable. He got up and paced to the dresser, pulling out a pair of boxers and stepping into them. He had to talk to his mate and it was best he wasn't naked doing it. His cock tended to rule his head.

He'd claimed River, drawn immediately to her and finding her eminently suitable, as his sire had insisted she would be. Solving the mystery of her determined independence had been a challenge he'd embraced, and his faith in her assuming the role of Alpha's mate hadn't been misplaced. He was proud of her, respected her, enjoyed spending time with her, and found her immensely pleasing in his bed. But was that love?

Oh, he was possessive, to a fault. But that was his

alpha talking, and he was committed to her for life. He liked her and would take care never to disparage those loftier feelings she appeared to have for him—even if he didn't understand them.

"I'm expected at the Sanctuary." River had pattered to the closet and was sliding hangers back and forth. A towel was wrapped around her small form, masking the view, and his fingers itched to tug it free. But he resisted the impulse, somehow wary.

When she turned to face him, clothing dangling from her hand, he searched her sweet features but found nothing to warrant his concern. Her comment about Desi hiding her feelings away flitted through his mind, but it was easier not to think about it—or draw a comparison. "Austin will take you."

"Sure." She tossed the garments on the rumpled bed and went to the dresser, picking out some underwear. The froth of lace caught his eye, so very different than the plain stuff she'd worn when he met her. His lovely little mate looked spectacular in sexy lingerie.

"Most of the women should be returning home in the next month or so."

"Most," she agreed, stepping into a pair of barely there blue panties and pulling them up underneath the towel. "A couple want to stay here, and then there are the ones who left voluntarily and caused a rift. All of them have accepted a placement. And Denise still isn't talking."

"You'll work it out," he said. And believed it. River had a way about her. Many of his pack members, with the exception of those like Tawny, found her to be unprepossessing at first, but the calmness she projected and her innate kindness soon won them over. And she could stand up for herself when needed.

The towel pooled around her hips as she fit the

matching bra around her breasts, her back to him. He crossed to her and took the ends from her fingers, efficiently hooking them up, and dropping a kiss close to his claiming mark. River tensed, and then grabbed for the flowing top she'd chosen, pulling it over her head and masking her face.

As she drew on the pants women wore, the ones that came just below the knees, she said, "Desi and I are meeting for dinner, so I'll see you later."

He frowned. He didn't think a day had gone by when they hadn't shared the evening meal. "I'd prefer if we ate together."

"Sorry." She looked up, her pants fastened, and brushed her hair back. "I promised."

"Then I'll have to accept it. But it's not to happen again," he teased, although his heart wasn't in it.

River's mouth set in a straight line before the plump curve of her bottom lip relaxed into a smile. "Yes, Alpha."

Every instinct told him to address whatever was transpiring. His wolf shook its head and paced. Jett wasn't a coward, preferring to face every life challenge head on, but he had no weapons—or the skill—to fight this particular battle. So he conceded. "See you later."

And for the first time since coming to live with him, his mate left without a kiss.

Chapter Eleven

Riding shotgun with Austin meant keeping her guard up and her mask firmly in place. River had nearly fallen apart in the bathroom upon realizing her feelings for Jett weren't returned, but her history of burying her issues had come to her rescue. Besides, her tears seemed frozen in some cauldron deep inside.

She focused on the screen of her phone, pretending something important kept her interest, and Austin stayed quiet and drove. When she let herself think about it, she realized that Jett hadn't made her any promises other than assuring her she was suitable as his mate. Love obviously didn't enter into the equation and she was foolish to think such a thing.

Attachment, yes. As Cass had insisted, their father and mother were attached. She could do attached. Jett liked her—a great deal—and he respected her. They were highly compatible sexually, although the idea of him touching her now... With a tiny shake of her head, she shoved the ridiculous thought away. Her body would melt beneath his expert touch as always and her next heat cycle would be mindless as always. And so it would go, month after month unless she conceived. She felt vaguely ill at the thought before tamping that down too. At least she could count on his fidelity because nature ensured it.

Taking deep breaths and calming her thoughts, she considered her lot. She had a life here outside of a loveless match with her Alpha, and once she had children, all this unrequited longing could be lavished upon them. He'd be a solid, protective father and she would make up for his inability to go that extra mile. Unless he might be able to love his offspring—just not her.

"Are you okay?" Austin's concerned voice broke into her reverie.

"What?" Had she made a sound to reflect her pain? "Oh, sure. I'm fine. A bit lost in thought."

"It's going to be a difficult visit."

"Not really. Mostly I'm concerned about the mated she-wolf."

"And rightly so. Do you get a sense if she's attached to the male?"

"She won't talk to anyone, including me."

"Maybe she fell for him."

"Like, in love with him?" Stab her in the heart.

Pulling up in front of the Sanctuary, Austin threw the vehicle into park. "Lots of claims go that way. Love grows out of the connection."

She wanted to lash out at him for giving her a glimmer of hope. She wasn't sure she had it within her to recover from the disappointment again. If disappointment even coined how she felt. "It'll make it even harder, then. And we don't even know the male's name."

"Chances are he's one of the deceased."

"Wouldn't she ... feel it? Like a loss of part of herself?"

"Good point. Maybe she'll talk to you today."

She forced a smile. "I'll give it a try. We can't keep her confined forever."

Moira opened the door to her, appearing far less worn and troubled. "It's good to see you, River."

"And you. How are you doing?"

"Better. I see Toni individually and a few of us have met to support one another in a group setting. Only time and a safe place is going to get most past what happened. And even then..."

She couldn't imagine. Her thoughts about being claimed and at another's mercy weren't even accurate and she'd been tortured by them, but these women had experienced far worse.

"How's Denise?"

Moira shrugged. "The same. I quit taking trays up to her, thinking she'd be forced to come out of her room, but I got worried she'd starve to death. Not that she's eating much of what I bring her."

"Who's her mate?" River had no idea what possessed her to ask.

"The—" The redhead blanched, her already pale skin turning nearly gray. She took a step back.

"Moira." River breathed the other woman's name. "What are you doing?"

Glancing over her shoulder, she reached for River's arm. "Can we talk in private?"

She let the female escort her to the kitchen and they huddled in a corner. Moira whispered, "Denise had no choice. He—the Regent—forced his claim on her, and you know what transpires with a mating heat. She was powerless against him."

"But why hide it? It's not her fault. Did she—did you—think the members of this pack would retaliate against her?"

"No. At least not once we got to know some of you. You've been nothing but kind. But Denise is resigned to her fate, and only wants to die."

"What?"

"Shh." Moira glanced toward the kitchen door. "She knows he's still alive and out there. There will be no escaping him. Claiming is for life, remember?"

"Then Jett will increase the efforts to track him down. And—" Holy crap. She was about to pronounce a death sentence on the Regent's head. A thought struck her. "Does she ... I mean, has she developed an attachment?"

Moira snorted. "There are a couple of female shifters I know that would get off on being humiliated and tormented and fall for their captor, but Denise isn't one of them. She's mortally afraid and shamed. And she's pregnant."

"Jeez."

"Exactly."

"You should have told us all of this before."

With a shrug, the other woman said, "I hoped the asshole would be tracked down and die in the struggle when your men caught up with him. It would have solved the dilemma. But as for Denise, I'm not sure she's ever going to talk to anyone again."

Her heart ached for Denise, but she had bigger worries. "I need to talk to Jett. What if that male finds her?"

Moira looked uneasy, shifting her weight and scanning the room. "How would he know where to look for her?"

"He'll know Jett freed you. Wolves are predators, Moira. And excellent trackers. Have you forgotten?"

Pressing a hand against her mouth, the redhead trembled. "I've been too messed up to think about it."

"Of course. I'm sorry. We'll put more men on the house as soon as possible." She texted the essentials to Austin who instantly responded, telling her to remain inside until further notice. She and Moira watched out the window, and she tried not to be furious at the other woman.

It felt like an eternity, but only minutes passed before two vehicles pulled up and disgorged several large males. Most faded into the surrounding shrubbery, but two mounted the steps. She recognized his step first. Jett strode into the house and came straight to her. "Are you okay?"

"I'm fine." And she was because he was here. The feeling of being safe around him hadn't changed.

"We're moving the majority of the women to various transfer points. They'll be met by members of their pack and taken home. Time is now of the essence. The ones who can't go back will be placed here with certain families until they're back on their feet."

"And Denise?"

"She'll be taken to a place more easily guarded, and looked after. We'll double our efforts to find her mate if he's still in the area. If not, well, she'll be moved across the country."

"You've gone to a great deal of trouble for us, Alpha. It's appreciated." Moira spoke up, wringing her hands.

"All of you put yourselves in danger by not disclosing Denise's connection. You put my mate and my sister in danger, your therapists." Jett's anger was cold and all the more frightening because of it.

The redhead bowed her head, as did several of the other women who'd filed in to find out what was happening.

"Austin will oversee things here. Kris is on his way. You're coming home with me, River. Cancel your dinner date with Desi."

"What?" She'd forgotten the fictitious meal. "I'll call her." And she would, but to bring the young woman up to date. There was nothing to give her reason to think that rogue leader knew about this place, but Desi had been here on a couple of occasions...

"Quit worrying, River. I have it under control."

"Sure." She threw Moira a glance and tried to smile before following her mate out to the vehicle. It felt as though hidden eyes watched her every move and she hurried along beside him.

He drove while she called Desiree, first apologizing for canceling on such short notice—to a confused response—and then sharing the latest. Their conversation took up the entire drive home and spared her further conversation with Jett.

"I'll be in my office. I need to oversee this. I've set the alarm. Stay inside and don't open the door."

Nodding, she rushed to the kitchen to make him something to eat and took the sandwiches and coffee in, setting it on the desk. He acknowledged her with a smile, and she refused to let it mean anything other than what he meant it to be. There was nothing wrong with an affectionate, mutually satisfying relationship. Apparently, shifters had them all the time—unless they didn't.

She made do with a glass of juice and a piece of toast at the island, her appetite gone. Poor Denise. Claimed by a monster. She shivered then squared her shoulders. She had a job to do.

Clearing her dishes away, she went to the meeting room where her files were spread out over the long table. She got everything in order, taking a couple of hours to do so, before heading up to bed. Jett's voice could be heard periodically and she wondered how long it would take to move everyone and get them safe. She sent out positive vibes and wished she had said goodbye.

Finding a pair of her old pajamas, she pulled them on and finished her nightly ritual of cleaning up. Once she was under the covers, her mind refused to be distracted any longer and reverted to considering her own issue. She pressed hard against the middle of her chest and thought about how selfish she was to allow something as stupid as a bruised ego to color her thinking. There were far worse things in life, as she'd just discovered.

So instead of the maudlin, she thought about her sister and how nice it would be to talk with her on a regular basis. She'd arrange for Austin to take her to see Marlene to discuss a business plan, perhaps tomorrow. Then there was the option of installing a new accounting program on the laptop she'd purchased. She had already called the employer she had lined up when she'd planned to run, and also the landlord of the small apartment, and couldn't think of anything else she'd missed.

Her brain ran down like a windup toy and time dragged. She heard Jett mounting the stairs, his tread heavier than usual. He was likely tired and she wouldn't give him any further angst to deal with tonight. That was what a good mate did.

Feigning sleep, she kept her breaths slow and measured as he moved around the room getting undressed and ready for bed. When he slid in behind her, and didn't draw her against him the way he always did when they prepared for sleep, she was profoundly grateful. The hollow feeling in her belly was simply that of hunger—she should have had more to eat for her makeshift dinner.

She knew the moment he fell into a deep slumber, attuned to so many of his behaviors. Dry-eyed, she stared into the dark and put her mind into solving equations until it was exhausted enough to quit chipping away at whatever it was that kept him from loving her.

Waking a short while later, she eased out of bed and made her way downstairs. The fridge didn't offer any helpful ideas as to what might help her sleep, and neither did the pantry. Dragging out the files again determined nothing to address, but at least enough time had passed that she could shower and get dressed and get on with her day.

****

His mate hadn't been in their bed most of the night. His wolf heard her slip out in the early hours and go downstairs to the kitchen and the meeting room. Jett supposed she was unsettled by the events of the day, not that he allowed himself to think about his perfidy. He couldn't feel what he didn't, and he wouldn't lie to her. There was no doubt, as evidenced by her marked pallor and wide eyes, that learning the Regent was Denise's mate had upset and worried her. The news had fucking well terrified him to know River was in the goddamn house and that rogue male could well be within stalking distance if not closer.

But she was fine, and the plan had unfolded perfectly, though had taken most of the evening to accomplish everything under his direction. Normally a hands-on kind of man, witness his participation in routing the rogue pack, he'd delegated the tasks and merely overseen the move of those female shifters. Kris had willingly taken on the most dangerous role, that of relocating Denise. Jett had stayed home to ensure River's safety.

Not that he'd spent any time in her company. He'd eaten the meal she'd brought him and waited a long time after completing his phone calls in the hope she'd be asleep when he went up to bed. It had killed him to keep his distance from her sleeping form, but it didn't feel right to take comfort from her when he hadn't offered her any earlier.

She moved quietly through their room, already dressed, and passed through the doorway. He opened his mouth to tell her good morning, and then swallowed the greeting. Time enough to put a good face on it once he'd showered the lack of sleep away. His wolf and his cock, both animals at heart, missed her physically, while the man wanted to hold her close and talk.

Awkward didn't cover it when he finally made it downstairs. River had made breakfast and he found his plate in the oven. Her dishes were in the dishwasher and she was in the meeting room poring over files and alternately peering at her computer screen.

"Thanks for breakfast." He saluted her with a piece of toast. "I see you're busy."

"I am." She spared him a glance before returning to her work. "I've called Austin. I have your mother's business plan ready, and she's expecting me."

"Good. That's great."

"Everything taken care of from yesterday?"

"Yes. All under control." Their easy, teasing way of relating had gone by the wayside. It bothered him more than he could explain. "River—"

A heavy hand rapped on the front door, and she jumped to her feet, stowing her laptop in its case. Gathering up her purse, she took the long way around the table—skirting him—and nearly fled to check the peephole, and then opened up to Austin.

"Morning!" The other male sounded enthusiastic and appeared as though he'd had plenty of rest, when Jett knew the opposite to be true. Austin had ferried at least four of the women to their meeting points. If he'd bothered to have a conversation with River instead of avoiding her, he could have told her that and arranged for someone else to drive her. She would never burden someone else.

"Sorry you drew taxi duty, Austin." His attempt at a humorous apology fell vastly short. River looked stricken and stammered her own apologies.

"It's fine." The male gave him a look fraught with numerous emotions, and smiled widely at River. "All set?"

"If you're sure…"

"Absolutely."

Flapping a hand in his direction, she rushed out with Austin right on her heels.

Refraining from punching his fist clear through the drywall, Jett slammed the door shut and locked it, before reversing the procedure and stepping out on to the porch. River was already in the SUV and Austin had one foot inside the vehicle. Jett scanned the yard, cursing his stupid reaction—his hurt—at being left without a backward glance.

Seeing no sign of anything untoward, he watched as they drove away, before retreating inside. Knowing he'd never get anything accomplished, he sat at his desk and brooded before banishing his bad mood. He needed a strategy to rebuild a bridge with his mate, and set to making plans.

****

Two blonde heads bowed over his mother's cluttered desk. His parent's hair was shot with silver, of course, but she and River shared a similar shade. Maybe it was true one claimed a mate similar to their mother, because Marlene and River also shared a number of superlative qualities. Caring, thoughtful, kind, intelligent, loving… "Hard at work?"

Both heads came up and a pair of eyes so similar to his own speared through him. He wondered what he'd done to deserve his mother's ire before catching River's brown-eyed stare. He tried a smile and she returned it, but there was something missing. A certain lack of warmth and a definite caution behind it.

"Morning, Jett. What can we do for you?" Marlene watched him steadily.

"I came to take my mate for lunch."

"I'm going with your mom and Desi. Seeing as I had to cancel our dinner date." Not a hint of regret infused River's tone. "Sorry."

"You're welcome to join us." His mother wasn't offering a welcome.

"Another time. I've brought two new males to replace Austin. Mikyle and Stephen." He'd seen Austin hovering in the shadows, vigilant as ever, but the man needed to be relieved. "They're to accompany you to lunch and bring River home. For dinner."

Complete and utter silence followed his autocratic response before both women nodded. He could tell his mother wanted to say something by the way her eyes narrowed, but she refrained. About to leave, he moved around the desk to his mate instead, and drew her to her feet.

Stiff as a board in his arms, she stared at him, then closed her eyes when he bent his head to take her mouth in a searing kiss. After an initial resistance, she softened and opened to him. When he released her, she swayed, her face slack and her eyes dazed. Satisfaction coursed through his veins and he shifted his hips to ease his hard cock. Their physical connection was as strong as ever and they'd soon be back on track.

Lowering her back into her seat, he chanced a look at his mother whose pleasant features were carefully blank. He knew that face, but he wasn't ten years old any longer. With a nod, he left the small office and wound his way through the various displays. Color and fine fabrics surrounded him, the sparkle of jewelry catching the eye and the air imbued with sultry scents. He hoped River spent more of his money here, because she was his to provide for and surely many of these items would make her happy.

He conveniently ignored the nagging voice in the back of his head suggesting things were far from joyful.

Chapter Twelve

She hadn't said anything to Marlene about the determination that Jett didn't feel the same way as she did, but the older woman intuited something wrong as soon as she entered the boutique.

"What's wrong, River?"

"Yesterday was a shock. To think that the rogue leader could be searching for his mate."

"Certainly. Though I understand Jett dealt with it."

"The women are moved," River agreed. "But if he wants Denise, he won't be far, right?"

Marlene pursed her lips. "If he's connected as with the usual style of claiming, he'll be around. And looking."

"Is there more than one style?" Like she didn't know.

"Every relationship is different, despite nature dictating the events following a claiming."

Marlene was doubtless referring to the sexuality piece, but River wanted to know more. The older woman had already told her that human-style love didn't necessarily follow a claim, but she wanted to torture herself further. "So you think that rogue will be attached?"

"She's his mate, no matter how he bent the rules. And so he's committed, and bound to her for life. If he strays, I fear for his soul."

"It doesn't sound as though he has one."

"Perhaps not, but even a rogue such as him can't circumvent nature."

So Jett would stay committed and loyal to her. She already knew that, so why keep picking? "Here's hoping he's found soon, then. Because everyone will be anxious until then, especially Denise."

"Are you sure that's all that's bothering you, honey?"

"Yes." She manufactured a breezy laugh. "You can't say it hasn't been a wild experience, me coming to this pack."

"And Jett is treating you well?"

"Absolutely." No lie. It wasn't his fault she wanted something he didn't have to give.

Marlene hesitated, and then gestured toward her office. "Then show me this plan of yours. Desi will be by later and we'll go for lunch. When do you have to be home?"

"No specific time. I mean, there's nothing there waiting for me." Realizing how that sounded, she hurriedly added, "Jett is busy and I'd rather stay busy than worry." *And fret.*

Marlene was a quick study and asked intelligent questions about the business plan. River wondered if the other woman truly needed her input, but soldiered ahead. Jett's arrival took her off guard, but she thought she carried it off, remaining calm and polite, hiding her pain—until he kissed her. He might as well have scooped her insides out with a spoon.

Gutted, she grimly rebuilt the new River, but not before her mother-in-law took notice.

"There is something wrong. Between you and Jett."

"There's nothing wrong, Marlene. We're both under a lot of stress and—"

"Bullshit. You're like Desi, all surface, no heart. What did my son do?"

"Nothing. Honest." True. And she put it out there with utter sincerity. He'd done nothing. It was all on her.

"Then I suggest you go home for dinner and fix that nothing."

She closed down the program after saving their input. "I'll send you the final outline tonight."

"Tomorrow is fine. You need to spend some time with Jett, seeing as you blew him off for lunch."

Couldn't the woman let it go? "Sure."

Desi waltzed in, wafting a delicate flower scent and modeling a slender sheath in azure blue. "You ready? I saw Mik and Stephen. Austin not around?"

"The others relieved him. He worked long hours yesterday."

"That makes sense. I'm glad most everything is taken care of, though Kris will be tied up for the foreseeable future."

"At least until they catch that rogue leader," River agreed.

They went for lunch to the same place as before, trailed by the big males Jett assigned. Over tall glasses of ice water, they perused the menu and almost as one decided on an exotic salad with grilled chicken.

"So, am I going to be an aunt?" Desi's smile seemed thin.

"Not this time." River's smile matched her sister-in-law's.

"She and Jett are having a problem."

Assailed on both sides, she whirled on the older woman. "I told you, Marlene. He didn't do anything wrong. It's all me and there's nothing to be done about it. Can you please leave it alone?"

Shaking her head, Marlene picked up her glass and took a sip. Desi stared. Aghast that she'd lost it, and on her mother-in-law, River scoured her brain for something further to say.

Marlene spoke first. "You too are a pair.

Allowing a male to get the best of you."

"Mom." Desi glared, and her hand gripped the tablecloth.

"Tahl's gone, dear. Probably mated by now. You need to—"

"Don't tell me what I need, Mother. You weren't the best role model." The younger woman crumpled up her napkin and tossed it on the table. "Sorry, River. For whatever's going on and for cutting lunch short. But I get to hear it at home and I sure don't need it repeated in public."

Desi strode out, and Mik levered up from his seat beside Stephen at a table by the door to follow her, presumably to her vehicle. Marlene calmly drank water.

"It's only been a few weeks you know." River had to say something in defense of Desi, seeing as she knew precisely how the younger woman felt.

"She's shut down, honey. Oh, the public face is perfect, but my baby girl is bone. And I can't have that. And I won't have it where you're concerned. You're both worth far more than moping because of a male."

"I can't—and won't—speak for Desi, but I will speak for myself. I'm claimed, Marlene. For life. And I'll have to figure a way to get through it. Me."

"You're not alone, River," she said quietly, her eyes now soft and gentle.

Oh, but I am. "I know that."

"Good."

Seeing Mik return, she said, "I'm not hungry. I think I'll head home and give these guys a break from babysitting me. Check your email for the plan—if you still want it."

"Of course, I want it, honey. I'm not angry with you, but I am concerned."

"You'll have it today." She forced a smile and

headed over to the males' table. "Sorry to interrupt your meal, but I really need to head home."

"No worries, River. Jett will be happy to see you." Stephen's broad face radiated nothing but good will.

She walked between them to their SUV and climbed into the back. Arriving home, Mik walked her to the door and Jett pulled it open. "You're home early."

Mik sketched a salute and headed back to the car as she went into the house. "Desi had to leave and your mother and I were … finished." That sounded about right. She hadn't been bossed around or pressured by a mother in nearly fifteen years, and she wasn't about to start now. No matter how well-meaning Marlene was.

"I've just eaten lunch. I've missed you. I have some business to deal with but we can spend the afternoon together."

"Sure. I have a couple of things to do first." It was easier if she didn't look directly at him. If he sort of hovered out there, barely within her line of vision, she could cope.

"I vote for a movie then. You look tired and need to relax."

He looked fatigued as well when she thought about it. "A movie sounds fine."

Carrying her case into the meeting room, she reviewed Marlene's business plan, going through it with a fine-toothed comb. Satisfied, she saved and sent a copy to the other woman, and then powered down. She was startled to notice that nearly an hour had passed.

"Finished?" How long had Jett been standing in the doorway, watching her?

"Yes. I'll go change."

"Need any help?" He was teasing but she picked up on some tentativeness.

It wasn't her job to soothe him, at least not with that. "Nope. I'll be down shortly."

"I'll make popcorn. Soda okay?"

"Fine." She slipped past him, intensely aware of the warmth of his big body and thought about their physicality all the way upstairs. She came to the conclusion about the time she tugged on a pair of yoga pants. Sex with him was tremendous—pleasurable and satisfying—so she'd take it. As for the rest of the time … well, she knew how Desi presented herself, and it was no hardship to enjoy Jett's company. Because she liked him too.

Her heart a hardening kernel in her chest, she went to join him.

Predictably, he'd chosen two movies. One was a pseudo-chick flick but with enough humor to presumably stave off any teeth grinding on his part, the other an action flick with lots of car chases and things being blown up. She'd seen them both, but it didn't matter. Jett made the effort, as he always did. "Doesn't matter to me."

"C'mon, River. Choose."

"The guy movie."

"Really?"

"Sure."

He called it up on the screen and patted the couch. "Sit with me."

Didn't she always? She plunked herself down and he pulled her close, like old times. If she tried hard, it felt like old times, before she'd opened her big mouth. The credits rolled and the opening scene filled the television and the sound echoed in the room.

"It's good to have some down time." He nuzzled her hair.

"It is." She desperately watched the movie unfurl.

He offered her popcorn but she declined, accepting the can of soda. Root beer had always been her favorite, but it tasted like soap today. She leaned over to set it down and he ran a hand down her back, making her shiver. Locking her chest down, she let her body take over and didn't resist when he slid that hand beneath her t-shirt and cupped her breast.

"I've missed this," he murmured.

Someone breathed their agreement, and he flicked open her bra to tease her exposed nipples. "Take your shirt off, sweetheart."

She complied and fell into the sensations of his clever fingers plucking her tight buds before his mouth covered one, and then the other to suck and nibble until her breasts ached. Her yoga pants and underwear joined her top on the floor, and his dark head fit between her widespread thighs as she fell back on the couch.

Whimpers and tiny moans escaped her lips as he placed an open-mouthed kiss on her pussy then lanced his talented tongue through the crevices to invade her channel. Circling her clit next, he tormented the tiny bundle of nerves until she bowed up to meet his touch, her hands scrabbling for purchase against the leather of the couch.

"God, Jett. Don't stop." Her voice pitched higher as he drove her up, pushing her over with a hard suck against his palate. She shrieked as the shudders of orgasm washed over her, and her heels drummed against the fabric.

He kissed his way up her stomach and between her breasts to the hollow of her throat, the rasp of his shirt and the rougher material of his jeans marking his progress. Freeing his cock, he notched it at her gate and fought for entry as she came down, her pussy clenching emptily.

"So fucking hot and wet. My little mate."

Screwing her eyes shut, willing back a torrent of tears, she took him deep into her body and he powered toward his own climax. Several hard strokes and he poured himself into her. She stared up as he threw his head back, his handsome face a picture of tortured pleasure. Her eyes drifted shut as he collapsed, much of his weight on top of her before he withdrew. River turned her head into the back of the couch and wept.

****

Standing awkwardly beside her, his dick throbbing and glistening with both of their juices, Jett watched his mate cry as though her heart was breaking. And maybe it was. He had no frame of reference, but her tears cut him up inside.

Grabbing a roll of paper towels, he cleaned up and tucked his cock away before gathering her against him. She tensed, and then curled in on herself. "What's wrong? Did I hurt you? River, tell me."

On a hiccupping sob, she swiped at her face and he offered a napkin. As she mopped at her face, she said, "Nothing's wrong. I'm fine. Just emotional."

Had he ever hesitated or flinched when facing his sire? His pack? The rogues? Even his mother? Never. So why now? "River…"

"Can I…" She gestured at the paper towels and he handed them over. She wiped her thighs and he cursed inwardly. He liked to take care of her himself and if he was honest, the sight of his mate filled with his cum met a primeval need for both him and his wolf.

"You're not pregnant."

"You know I'm not."

He did. Her heat had passed and he'd bought the test himself, just in case. Two of them. Human pregnancy tests worked the same for shifters. "So why so emotional?"

"I don't know. Female stuff."

She wasn't telling him the truth and it was time they hammered it out. "You're upset because I can't tell you that I love you."

Shaking her head, she looked everywhere but at him.

"Things changed the minute we had that conversation, sweetheart."Her eyes popped wide and a small hand crept up to press against her lips. She shook her head. "Don't. Please. Don't talk about it," she mumbled.

"We have to talk about it. Goddamn it, River. Men have a hard time talking, but I'm willing to do it for you. I want our connection to go back to the way it was before I … before I hurt your feelings."

With an audible gulp, she replied, "You did hurt my … feelings. You bruised my pride. So I'm emotional."

"For how long? Sweetheart, things can't continue this way. We were doing so well together. I don't want you to cry every time we have sex, and we have to present a united front. My mother sensed something was off today." The pile of crap that tumbled from his mouth couldn't be recalled.

His mate's petite form shook visibly and her tears dried before his eyes. "Screw you, Jett Reeves. Screw you and your time limit. It'll take as long as it takes. And as for the *sex,* you'll just have to wait for my next heat when you'll get all the fucking you want—without the tears."

Her words provoked him but he pushed down his anger. "Sweetheart—"

"Don't call me that. Ever again." She clambered to her feet, a naked Fury, with her eyes blazing golden fire and her fingers curled into claws. She was close to shifting and his wolf raged against his skin. "I'm your mate, and I'll fulfill those duties. For life. But don't you call me that. I'm nowhere near in your heart."

Not trusting himself to react in a way that could spell an irretrievable blow to their connection, he made himself back off. "I hear you, River. I'll give you the time you need."

Tugging his cell from his pocket, he hit a number. "Mik? How long for you to get back here? I need you to stay with River. Stephen can spell you."

Resisting the desperate urge to pull her indignant, furious body into his arms and make it all go away, he nodded instead. "I'll see you ... later."

****

How dare he? Standing there completely clothed and put together while she sprawled on the couch, naked, and a hot, wet mess. She'd accommodated him sexually—not a hardship. They'd continued their physical relationship. And then he'd wanted to *talk*? He couldn't give her a day to come to terms with the fact their relationship was one-sided? Impatience—or coldness—must run in the family. And she had to remain in this family until death do them part.

Even that awful thought didn't distract her from her rage. If that burned out what would she have left? A frigid detente was in the cards for at least three weeks each and every month of each and every miserable year of the rest of her life. Lovely.

Jett had watched implacably as she stormed past him to head up to their room, something that was going to change lickety split. She'd choose one of the guest rooms down the hall and they could cohabitate here when her heat flared. It'd be like taking medicine, albeit a great tasting one with wonderful side effects.

179

Her laughter was punctuated by shuddering sobs as washed herself at the sink before yanking on some clothes. She gathered up armfuls of fabric and toted her belongings down the hall to the furthest bedroom, tossing everything on the bed. She made several trips before her Alpha called up to her.

Willing her angst into compliance, she sent down to see Mik dropping a duffel beside the door and Jett explaining the alarm system. "She's not to go outside without one of you. I'll check in regularly."

"Got it, boss." Mik noticed her and cocked his head. "Hey, River."

"Hi, Mik. Back to babysitting me?"

"Looks like it, not that I mind!"

"I promise not to cause you any trouble," she said, knowing she looked worse for wear and the young male had noticed.

"River isn't feeling well." Jett wasn't lying, and he probably knew it. "So, are you set?"

"Sure. I'll call if anything seems off, sir. Where do you want me to sleep?"

"There's a safe room off the kitchen. Closed security screens, the usual."

"Are you expecting trouble?" Mik stood straighter, obviously not fearful, but alert.

"Just being careful. That rogue leader is out there."

Jett hoisted a duffel of his own, and she fixed a polite smile on her face. She had no idea where he was going and wouldn't let it matter. "Goodbye, River."

"Bye." She waited until the door closed behind him before making an excuse to Mik. "Help yourself to anything in the kitchen. I'm going to lie down."

"You take care, River. And let me know if you need anything."

As if anyone had what she needed. "I will."

She had a room to straighten and make her own, and then she'd sleep. Exhaustion didn't cover the way she felt. Maybe she'd have a nap before she put things away.

****

Waking, she wasn't sure where she was, before memories crashed around her and yanked her into her reality. The house felt empty without Jett, despite knowing a bodyguard was on the main floor. She felt around for her cell phone and studied the screen. A couple of texts from Desi and one missed call from Marlene, a few voicemails from other members of the pack. Some of the females wanted her to stop by for a visit. Maybe when she could fake her way through an hour or two. What had he called it? A united front. She bet he was regretting his claim.

Hanging up clothes and setting smaller items in the dresser, she paused in the middle of folding a gauzy nightgown. Her former Alpha's grown children were in Jett's age group, so what was that edict about fidelity? Maybe it didn't apply to alphas. Maybe Jett was out there right now getting his needs met.

Refusing to label it jealousy, she coaxed her reaction into a more palatable emotion—anger. Shifters didn't carry disease, so she had no concern on that front. And if it meant he'd stay away for periods of time, surely that would make it easier for her.

Her belongings stowed, she went in search of her laptop, and began the arduous task of installing her new accounting program. Numbers were easy for her, following instructions written by some person who spoke code, not so much. Mik poked his head in to offer a meal, but she refused—nicely. He brought a cup of weak tea and renewed his well wishes before retreating. Probably didn't want to catch what was going around.

Entering the pack's books took her well into the night before her vision blurred and her head ached too much to continue. River dragged herself up to her room and collapsed.

****

Tahl's home was comfortable and clean. That about summed it up. The main thing it lacked was River, and Jett found it extremely difficult to come to terms with. He explored the entire dwelling before putting away a few groceries he'd picked up, and then tossed his duffel in the master bedroom.

He knew River wasn't sleeping in theirs. He'd heard her pacing back and forth to one of the other rooms, and panic momentarily froze his thoughts, thinking she was packing, before he spoke to distract Mik. He told the man he was leading the task force to hunt down the rogue leader to put an end to the issue once and for all. In fact, had he not been mated, he'd have been doing just that earlier.

The young male came highly recommended by Tahl, and Stephen was no slouch either. He wanted River well protected in his absence while he did his job and gave her the time she needed. Though somehow he doubted there was enough time in the world. But he hadn't become Alpha by being indecisive, and she really hadn't left him any choice.

His cell vibrated and he nearly dropped it in his haste to drag it from his pocket. His anticipation wavered when he saw the name on the screen. "Yes, Mom?"

"Did I catch you at a bad time?"

"No. I'm organizing another push to find that rogue."

"You're not with River?"

"No."

"What did you do, son? Oh, I know she says you did nothing, but in my experience—"

River said he'd done nothing? He supposed it was true. "Stay out of it, Mom. We're working things out."

"She's hollow, Jett. I'm worried. She's not like me or a lot of the other females."

What was that supposed to mean? It didn't matter. This was between him and his mate. "If we need your help, I promise to call. Now, let me work."

His cell signaled again almost immediately and he sighed. "Mom."

"Uh, no. It's Tahl."

"Oh. You got my message?"

"A few minutes ago. You're staying in my house?"

"Until we catch the Regent."

"Is your place a target?"

His chest clamped as though a giant hand had clutched it. He'd left River alone. No, she wasn't alone. Mik was with her. "I don't think so, but River distracts me and this is serious."

"Mik brought me up to date when I suggested he offer to watch over your family. Pretty messed up, that thing with Denise. She was nearly catatonic when Kris carried her out of that room."

"Totally messed up. How's it going with you and Peyton?" Silence. Jett counted at least five seconds. "Hello? Tahl?"

"I'm here." A chuckle sounded. "I think I might want to dodge a bullet, but I've set things in motion. Expectations and all."

"What?"

"She's not who I thought she was."

"What female is, Tahl?" Who knew his sweet little River would want to bite the hand that fed her?

Knowing it was his own fucked up thinking that fueled his reaction, he changed gears. "Sorry. I just meant there are depths to everyone and it takes time to know a person." *Like the time you gave River before you spirited her away from her home.* He wasn't going to regret that. He'd done the right thing. River was right for him, and he for her.

Tahl was mumbling about princesses and entitlement. "I didn't see past her looks, Jett."

"So you don't want to claim her? You'd come home?" Good thing no one was listening in, because his desperation was palpable. He'd missed his lieutenant.

"I'm trying to figure out a graceful way to bow out without souring relations between the packs."

"Tell Ashton our situation has deteriorated and I've ordered you home."

"And make you look weak? I don't think so. I'll find a way."

"See that you do. Sooner the better."

"How's Desiree?"

Misery loves company, wasn't that the term? "My mother says she's hollow."

"Fuck."

He felt a little better. "Keep me updated."

"Jett? What's really going on with River?"

"Saw through my subterfuge, did you? I can't betray her by telling you, buddy. But it was me who fucked up. And no way to fix it."

"You have a lifetime to try."

Maybe his feelings would transform to match River's over time. If she didn't succeed in shutting him out.

He called one of the teams to establish their whereabouts before heading there to join them. Canvassing all the likely places a rogue might take cover in was time-consuming and another pair of legs and eyes wouldn't hurt. Eventually, they'd drive the man out, ahead of the sweep.

Chapter Thirteen

It might have been the noises that dragged River from her sleep. Stifling a groan, she lifted up on one elbow and listened, but the breaking of glass—or whatever it was—didn't sound again. But still, hadn't there been a thud, too? She peered around by the aid of a nightlight but saw nothing.

She was still wearing the same long-sleeved t-shirt over the leggings she'd donned after the impromptu sexual escapade with Jett. Best she think of it that way. Her bra hung loose over her arms and she twitched it down one sleeve to toss it on the floor. Mik would have to be offended by the sight of unrestrained breasts. Ha.

Halfway down the stairs, relying on the light spilling from the outside lamps, she wobbled with one foot hovering over the tread. Living in a safe, protected pack, despite all her groundless fears about males and claiming, had softened her instincts. Her wolf was wide awake and howling for her to stay alert. She opened her mouth to call for Mik before swallowing his name. She didn't even have her phone with her. Stupid. Really stupid.

Quietly, she reversed her path and raced back up, clutching the railing. She nearly turned toward the master before catching herself and running along to her room. Her cell should be on her dresser. She grasped it in a sweaty palm and it flickered on in response to her fingerprint. Stabbing at Jett's icon, she listened to it ring before the sound of his voice coincided with a growl and a huge hand batted the phone across the room.

She screamed, a wild, high-pitched sound she wouldn't have believed herself capable of, but the big male in her room was the stuff of nightmares. First of all, she couldn't believe she hadn't scented him. He'd clearly been living rough or bathing wasn't a personal habit. The poor visibility thrown by the tiny bulb plugged into the wall created ghoulish crannies over the planes of his face, and his swatch of dark hair hung in lank spirals.

"Who did you call, bitch?" He grabbed a handful of her shirt and shoved her into the wall. "Who?"

"My mate," she gasped, wondering if it would be the last time she would refer to him.

"Fuck. Fuck me. You bitches always ruin things." He threw her on the bed in a frightening display of strength and crossed to the phone, stomping it into the floor. "I could have stayed here, waited for him and surprised him. With you to keep me entertained and him under control."

River tried to think what she could get her hands on that might keep the Regent at bay. For there was no doubt in her mind he was the rogue leader being hunted. She inched her way toward the lamp on the nightstand, but a heavy hand forestalled her.

"Move and I'll break your arm. You'll do as a hostage, and it doesn't matter what shape you're in."

She froze and watched his shadowy form as he moved to flick on the light. Cleaned up, he would probably exude a caveman appeal, but all she could see was evil. He looked around and spied her bra, picking it up and motioning her to him. Somehow, she made herself get off the relative safety of the bed and move.

"Put your hands out."

Numbly, she complied, and he bound her wrists together, then hooked a finger behind a piece of strap and dragged her along. He glanced into each room until gaining the master suite. Stepping inside, he shoved her to sit on the bed while he yanked open first the closet, and then a couple of dresser drawers.

"Trouble in paradise, girl? You and your mate sleep in separate rooms? I wonder why that is." Moving quickly, he stripped off his filthy clothes, laughing when she averted her eyes, and pulled on some of Jett's things.

"Where's the money kept? And don't stall, bitch. We're leaving in three minutes, long before your mate can get here. If you delay me..."

"My purse. Downstairs."

"Go."

She clambered to the base of the stairs, her balance hampered by her tied hands, and headed to the meeting room, counting off the seconds in her head. "Were you looking for the Sanctuary?"

"What? I don't need no church." He dumped the contents of her purse out and grabbed the cash and cards from her wallet.

"The Sanctuary. Where the females you ... held are staying."

More seconds ticked by as the Regent's big frame froze in place. Only his head moved as he turned it to fix a death stare on her. "Take me there."

"Are you wanting Denise?" If he was distracted long enough, maybe he wouldn't notice that over three minutes had passed. Something in her head clicked, like a switch, and she felt Jett as though he was right inside of her.

He was on her instantly, taking hold of her hair and yanking her head back. His sour breath nearly made her gag, his face was so close to her own. "Did she tell you?"

"That you're her mate? How else would I know? She said you would come."

He let go so suddenly, she sidestepped to regain her footing. Something that looked remarkably like pain twisted his heavy features. "We've been looking."

We? "Is someone else here?"

He shook her, grabbing her shoulder. "What other females are there?"

"I don't remember their names, but there are some who went with ... your males willingly?"

"Francine? Sherri?"

"Maybe. I'm not good with names."

"We're wasting time. C'mon." He pushed her toward the door. "Take me to her."

"She's pregnant." It felt like the worst betrayal in the world, but it was all she had.

He slowed his pace. "Is she okay?"

"Yes. Though she's refusing medical care. Maybe she doesn't trust us."

"I'll take care of her. My pup will be fine." His fanaticism burned past the softer side she'd glimpsed—mistaken for actually caring. Denise was merely a means to an end.

Four hundred and ninety-seven seconds had elapsed since he'd announced his time frame, and she hoped it was enough. If Jett had recognized her call as one for help. A shiver overtook her and she bit her lip as the rogue drove her ahead of him, past the prone form of Mik.

"Mik!" She slowed to look at him.

"He's dead. Nothing you can do. Get moving." Without mercy, she was shoved toward the doors opening onto the pool. Shards of glass shimmered against the tile floor.

"I don't have any shoes."

"You'll heal."

She tried to take care, but several tiny pieces ground into the ball of one foot, and a larger one caught her across the instep. She cried out and all hell broke loose.

Several dark figures swarmed toward the rogue male who raised a baton he'd picked up from somewhere. Her fingernails pricked savagely, trying to elongate into claws. River ducked, but the blow connected with a splinter of agony, and her world went dark.

****

"River." Something cool touched her brow. "River."

Her eyelids were simply too heavy to lift, and she sank back into the current to drift along.

"She was nearly back, I swear." A familiar, feminine voice, thick with tears, protested somewhere close by.

"She'll wake when she's ready, Cass. Leave her for now." Another familiar voice, this one male, cajoled.

"Please, River. I know you're ready now. Please."

The plea was too hard to resist, and somehow, she pried open her eyes. A young, pretty face greeted her, the brown eyes popping wide and a huge smile gracing the wide mouth.

"You're back! I knew it. Jett!"

Wincing at the exuberant scream, she cautiously looked around, though it hurt to even move her eyeballs. As she lifted a hand to her head, the door flew open and a huge male shifter advanced into the room.

"River!"

Her name had to be River, an interesting choice. She felt she should know these people, all of whom, even the older man hovering in the corner, looked so happy to see her. She stared at the handsome, young male. A shifter. Wait. What?

"How are you, sw—River? The nurse is coming with something in case you're hurting. And the doctor will be by soon."

The door eased wide again, and a nurse, bearing a syringe, moved to her. She shone a light into her eyes and checked the machines surrounding the bed. "Your pupils are the same size, so the brain injury is healing. Blood pressure and oxygen stats look okay. Do you have pain?"

"My head hurts."

"I'll put this in your IV, but I'd like to ask you a few questions first."

Was this like a reward? Her sarcastic thought made her wrinkle her brow, a mistake because that really hurt.

"You pulled your stitches a little. They're a long way from being healed," the nurse advised. "What's your name?"

"River. At least that's what they're calling me."

"Oh. Okay. Last name?"

A tendril of fear snaked up her spine. "I don't know."

"That's fine. You sustained a hit to the head, a big one, and sometimes things get muddled. Do you remember?"

Thinking back, she couldn't recall—anything. The fear morphed to full blown panic and the machines beeped and she struggled to sit up.

"Easy." The handsome male set his hands on her shoulders, engulfing them in his palms and gently urged her to lie back. His touch lit something inside her that drove the panic back.

She took a deep breath. "I'm scared. I don't remember anything."

"None of us are surprised, or disappointed, sweetheart. The surgeon warned us that short term memory loss isn't uncommon with this kind of injury. Like the nurse said. Let her give you the medicine, and rest. When you wake up, it'll be better. I promise."

Somehow, she believed him. The young woman was weeping quietly and the older male appeared lost, but she had faith in this man. "Okay. But what's your name?"

Despair flashed over his face before he smiled, his wintry, blue eyes softening. "Jett."

"And how do I know you?"

"Why don't we wait for the next time you wake?"

She wanted to know now, urgently, but whatever was in that syringe was potent. She succumbed to its pull.

****

"Her skull was fractured and her brain sustained an injury, Mr. Reeves. As I've explained. The pressure has been released, and she is healing. All the tests reveal normal progress. If anything, quicker than I'd expect, although that's not uncommon with shifters. My task to play down that healing and explain away the anomalies in her blood was the difficult part, before we could move her from hospital. She'll be fine."

"But she doesn't know me. Or her immediate family!"

"That isn't uncommon either. I don't expect her to ever recall the immediate events leading up to the blow. As for the other, things will come back. She can speak, and her hearing wasn't affected. Her level of motion is good, including her fine motor skills. We took out the catheter and the IV. She's doing very well."

Jett put his head in his hands. "She nearly died."

"But she didn't. And she needs her mate in good shape to support her in her recovery. How much weight have you lost? How much sleep? Living in her room, trying to rest in a chair, and skipping meals isn't healthy."

"And yet she woke the minute I left to get a coffee."

"It's normal for males to be so distraught when their mate is in danger, Mr. Reeves. But you've surpassed everything in my experience. So either you aren't dealing with the guilt or you love her so much you aren't thinking at all clearly. Maybe it's a combination of both."

Jett looked up at the medical man, another shifter who had been happy to help River. Yes, he'd breathed, slept, and eaten guilt for weeks, since seeing his mate crumble beneath the cruel blow the rogue male had laid on her. But the sense of loss—if this was love, it should have killed him. Except it hadn't.

"She's my life. And I didn't know until I nearly lost her."

"Then take hold of your second chance with both hands and don't let go." The doctor rose and rubbed his own hands together, as if in sympathy. "I have to get back to the hospital. I won't need to check on my patient again unless the nurse detects anything untoward. Bringing in a therapist is a good idea too."

"Thank you." When had those two simple words meant so much?

"Doing the job I was trained for. And happy I could do it. River seems pretty special."

Jett showed the man out and shut the door, leaning his forehead against it. He had to gather himself and head up to see his mate. He owed her some explanations and the entire truth, as much as she could handle at one sitting.

"Hey." Tahl set an arm around his shoulders and gave him a side hug. "How're you doing?"

"For a dumb ass, as well as can be expected." His friend had returned a few days after the battle by the pool, quietly taking over and keeping pack business running while Jett watched over River. Mik hadn't died, but he wasn't going to be the same old Mik, either, and Tahl had looked after the man. Tahl also arranged for Cassandra and her father to come and generally did what a lieutenant—and a best friend—did.

"Is she going to be all right?"

"The surgeon says so. He figures her memory will return in bits and pieces as she's surrounded by the familiar, or even in a flood. I thought about taking her back to her home, but Reginald is against it. He thinks happier times will jog her memory quicker and be kinder." He snorted. "He doesn't know what happened between us."

"Nothing happened, Jett. She fell in love and you didn't reciprocate—or thought you didn't, at the time. You didn't lead her on, which would have been far crueler. Maybe you handled it badly, and you were insensitive, but females have a huge capacity for forgiveness if you give them reason."

"When did you get your psychiatrist papers? Or lose your dick? Who are you and what have you done with my friend, Tahl?" More frightening, everything his friend had said made perfect sense.

"I talked with someone, a professional, and kept an open mind. Because I have some amends of my own to make."

With an effort, Jett shut his mouth, watching the other male stride away. Scrubbing a hand through his hair, he winced and headed off to clean up before River woke. He avoided his office, where his mother lurked, unable to face her. She was hesitant to see River, as well, and he suspected she'd overstepped, as she was wont to do.

When he entered the master suite, now a hospital

room for all intents and purposes, it was dim and quiet. Cass read in the corner, under a small lamp, but Reginald wasn't there. She looked up and closed her book, keeping a finger inside to mark the page.

"She's starting to stir. The nurse said to call if she wants a bedpan, but she isn't due more pain meds for another couple of hours."

"I'll carry her to the bathroom." His mate wasn't going to endure another minute of humiliation if he could help it. "Can I have some time alone, Cass?"

"Of course. I'm sorry she woke when you'd stepped out, but I felt her so close to the surface."

So had he, which is why he'd climbed the stairs in two long strides. "It's fine. She woke up. That's all that matters."

He dragged her chair closer to the bed and waited for River to open her eyes, studying her bruised face and slender body. She'd be weak too, though that would pass. If only she could remember...

"Is it morning?"

"Late afternoon. You needed the sleep."

She blinked at him, chocolate-brown eyes surrounded by multicolored contusions, and gave him a small smile. "Who are you, Jett?"

"Your mate."

A tiny furrow appeared between her brows and he saw her breathing speed up, though she visibly tried to control it. "Shifters. That's right. I might not have my memory, but I recognized them like I knew what a nurse looked like. She's a shifter too. And the doctor."

"We're a talented community. You're an accountant."

"Really? Maybe that's why I think in numbers, like how far you're sitting from me, and how many windows in this room... What do you do in this pack?"

"I'm the Alpha."

A quick inhale of air and she was back to breathing too hard.

"Don't feel surprised. You're a special she-wolf, River. I knew it the moment I laid eyes on you, and why I claimed you."

"I don't remember."

"It was an unorthodox claim. I've thought about it and it was like something in medieval times." He explained how the claiming had come about, lowering his voice as he mentioned her use of supplements.

"I did that? To avoid being claimed? Wow. There's gotta be some history there for us to talk about. If you know it."

"I do. You shared it with me and we laid it to rest. I swear."

"That's good then." She asked, "What's the penalty for contravening pack law?"

"It varies from pack to pack," he said, evasively.

Tilting her head, he saw a faint wince, but she put her hand up when he moved to press the call button. "It's okay. I have to remember not to move too quickly." She closed her eyes for a second and frowned, and then focused on him. "Did you ... did you *spank* me?"

"Something I regretted later, honestly. I've learned a lot of things and do things differently since we met. Damn it, River. I hadn't counted on that being your first memory."

"It must have made an impression."

"I'd hoped other things would have made a better impression."

"Maybe they did and I haven't gotten there yet."

"Oh, we got there before." He wanted to call the words back but it was too late.

River laughed and winced. "Oh, jeez. No

laughing either. But, your face…" She giggled weakly and then sobered. "Did we talk like this? Before?"

"A lot of the time. Once you loosened up."

"And accepted my fate?"

"It took a while," he admitted. "You were dead set against claiming."

"You are very persuasive. My wolf knows you and is champing to get to you."

His damn cock perked up and he moved to hide it. "You haven't shifted."

"No? Is that usual? Wait, it is. I remember learning about it at home. Females don't shift unless under extreme duress. My mother talked to me…"

"Cass, your little sister, is waiting, and your dad. Did you want them to come in? They'll want to tell you about your mom."

"Later, though I think Cass shouldn't wait too long. But I want to know more about you. About us."

"It might be too much to handle, but I believe we are fated mates. Our connection is eerie. There were other instances, but the night you were … hurt, I was on my way to you because I felt your terror. I heard you in my head and in my heart."

"That doesn't happen often." She closed her eyes and rested for a while. He waited patiently for her to process and gain some strength.

"So you and I are right for one another, despite a less than auspicious start. Things were going well, I take it?"

"Yes. You've been through your first heat, and were settling in very well. Helping out and most welcome in the pack. We've had you working. My mother loves you and so does my sister."

"Desi? Tall and dark like you?"

"She is. How much do you recall?"

"Impressions. I think I like her, though she's sad." She stared at him. "I'm sad. Or I was."

"With a mate like me, it's no doubt you'll be sad sometimes. But you were happy, and you told me so." He couldn't make himself say the rest and wished for the nurse to come in, or Cass, even his mother. *Coward.* In a burst, her gaze steady on him, he said, "You told me you loved me—and I couldn't reciprocate."

River's hands flew up to her temples and she whimpered, so quietly his wolf primarily heard her and the beast retreated to curl up into a ball. Jett listened to instinct and climbed onto the narrow hospital bed beside her, crowding her and drawing her close.

He spoke against her temple, into the short, silky hair growing in where they'd shaved her scalp, past the bandage denoting the injury that so nearly took her life. "I couldn't reciprocate then, sweetheart. Not then, but only because I didn't know what you were talking about. Absolutely no fucking idea. But I know now. And almost losing you nearly killed me. Way past the attachment of mates. River, sweetheart, I love you much I can't get a deep breath most times."

"Sweetheart." The word sounded strangled as if she could barely speak it.

"I called you it before I understood why. It's more than an endearment. To me. I've been praying you'll forgive me."

"Do you promise?"

"Promise?" He carefully moved her so he could see her face, her brutalized, beautiful face. "I'll promise anything if I know I can keep it."

"Do you promise that you love me? That it's not something you're saying so I'll get better?"

He choked on something in his throat. Not a sob. He'd had softer feelings beaten from him before he was eight. And his eyes weren't wet either. "I promise."

Somehow, the simple responses, the humble words, meant more than all the flowery speeches.

"I forgive you." The whisper was the last of her strength because her body went slack in his arms and for one agonizing moment, he thought...

But her chest lifted and fell beneath the fabric of her gown, festooned with bouncing lambs and tiny bunnies. Marlene had brought in a variety to choose from and didn't contain her delight when he picked this one.

He held her until his arm went to sleep and the pins and needles tormented him. He deserved far worse.

Epilogue

She could hear Cassandra calling Andrew's name as she chased him across the yard. Her first born could keep four adults busy at any given time with his over-the-top energy and crazy antics. He was bright—too bright for nearly three, and River reflected that Marlene had warned her. Andrew was already reading and doing simple sums. And he required far less sleep than was fair.

She and her mother-in-law maintained a cordial relationship, and River knew the older woman would choose for it to be deeper, the way it started out, but there was something different about Marlene. Something Fae. River wasn't enamored with the paternalism that ruled the shifter packs, but the other woman would dismantle it, and without anything to replace it. If she knew anything, River knew not to mess with nature.

She left it to Desi to deal with her mother, especially where Tahl was concerned. Tahl, come back to the pack and never far from Desiree—who didn't appear to notice he existed.

"His grandfather went for a nap." Jett stretched out beside her on a lounger, the pool sparkling beyond him. His scent enveloped her and she breathed him in. "Reginald keeps saying he's glad he had girl pups."

"*Your* father can't keep up for an afternoon."

"And he's had more experience with boys," her mate conceded.

"But not like Andrew."

"True. He's destined for greatness if we can keep him pointed in the right direction." He reached out and set his hand on her belly. "Do you want to find out what this one is?"

"No. The Goddess wouldn't be so cruel to give us another Andrew. This baby will be more sedate. Like

Bella." Their eighteen-month-old daughter slept in the shade of a tree, sprawled out luxuriously, tired after hours in the pool with her daddy. Bella was quietly smart and tended to get her own way because she wasn't as obvious as Andrew.

"And then there's the next one after this." He smiled, and despite her heat having fizzled to nothing the instant she conceived, her core moistened. He only had to look at her sometimes for her to crave him, the way any woman craves the man she loves. Jett lifted a brow at the way her nipples peaked and pointed beneath the fabric of her bikini. Her breasts were fuller now, considerably larger, and she knew he liked them though would never compare from earlier times.

"Another one? If *you* carry it. And bear it."

"I would if I could, sweetheart. Andrew made you scream, and not in a good way, and Bella made you work too hard, as well. I hate feeling powerless and unable to intervene and help you."

"You complained about having no feeling in your hand for days. And you keep showing people the teeth marks in your forearm."

He took hold of her waist and without any apparent effort, swept her to lie on top of him. She splayed across him with no regard for Cass's sensibilities, figuring her sister's education was far superior to her own at that age.

"I like your touch. Any of it," he said.

She loved the feel of him, that broad, muscled chest with its soft fur against her skin. The long, thick length of his cock hardened against her mound, and she hitched up a little to work it between her folds. Only the thin material of her suit kept him from sliding right inside. That and the definite possibility that their son would burst on the scene with his uncanny timing. The loving he'd interrupted…

"Three babies, Jett. Three. And then you'll be making a trip to your friend the doctor."

He blanched but nodded. "You're sure? If you make the visit, your heats will stop."

"They've diminished and are manageable. I don't find them incapacitating. " She pumped her hips against him, enjoying his involuntary hiss. "Maybe because you've proven to be more than capable of assuaging them. Fully."

"Wench."

"Snuggle buns."

On a groan, he hugged her tight. "I've give you a sample of assuaging tonight, once the kids are in bed—asleep."

"I'd like more than a sample."

"Deal."

They relaxed under the hot sun, a cool breeze making it bearable.

"I love you, sweetheart."

After a proper time count, she replied, "Love you back."

The End

www.allysonyoung.com

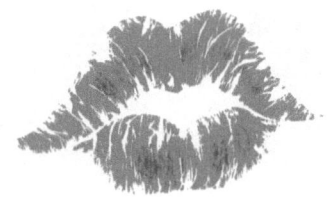

EVERNIGHT PUBLISHING ®

www.evernightpublishing.com

www.ingramcontent.com/pod-product-compliance
Lightning Source LLC
Chambersburg PA
CBHW022104170626
46808CB00002B/590